W9-DGX-874

Dear Reader,

I live in a part of North America with four definite seasons. This book was written during the early spring, a time of tender new grass, yellow daffodils and bright tulips. It is a time when I can once again sit in the yard with my face lifted to the sun, but also a time when furious storms can sweep in from nowhere.

Isn't love just a little bit like that? This nanny and her prince are both about to discover a season of the heart: where storms brew and pass, where things too-long dormant bravely bloom again and where every day becomes fresh and hope-filled.

To know spring—or to experience love—is to be at the very center of the miracle that is life.

I invite you to join Prudence and Prince Ryan as they discover the miracles of the most exciting season of all.

Best wishes,

Cara Colter

By Royal Appointment

You're invited to a royal wedding!

From turreted castles to picturesque palaces—
these kingdoms may be steeped in tradition,
but romance always rules!

So don't miss your VIP invite to the most
extravagant weddings of the year!

Your royal carriage awaits…

Next month another royal meets his match in

Matrimony with His Majesty
by
Rebecca Winters

CARA COLTER
The Prince and the Nanny

By Royal Appointment

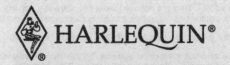

TORONTO • NEW YORK • LONDON
AMSTERDAM • PARIS • SYDNEY • HAMBURG
STOCKHOLM • ATHENS • TOKYO • MILAN • MADRID
PRAGUE • WARSAW • BUDAPEST • AUCKLAND

If you purchased this book without a cover you should be aware
that this book is stolen property. It was reported as "unsold and
destroyed" to the publisher, and neither the author nor the
publisher has received any payment for this "stripped book."

ISBN-13: 978-0-373-03940-1
ISBN-10:   0-373-03940-9

THE PRINCE AND THE NANNY

First North American Publication 2007.

Copyright © 2007 by Collette Caron.

All rights reserved. Except for use in any review, the reproduction or
utilization of this work in whole or in part in any form by any electronic,
mechanical or other means, now known or hereafter invented, including
xerography, photocopying and recording, or in any information storage
or retrieval system, is forbidden without the written permission of the
publisher, Harlequin Enterprises Limited, 225 Duncan Mill Road,
Don Mills, Ontario, Canada M3B 3K9.

All characters in this book have no existence outside the imagination of
the author and have no relation whatsoever to anyone bearing the same
name or names. They are not even distantly inspired by any individual
known or unknown to the author, and all incidents are pure invention.

This edition published by arrangement with Harlequin Books S.A.

® and TM are trademarks of the publisher. Trademarks indicated with
® are registered in the United States Patent and Trademark Office, the
Canadian Trade Marks Office and in other countries.

www.eHarlequin.com

Printed in U.S.A.

Cara Colter, a journalism graduate, lives in British Columbia, Canada, on an acreage she shares with eight horses, a cat and her very own prince, Robert.

"A prince doesn't always look like a prince," Cara says. "Sometimes they come driving old pickup trucks. Like the heroine of this story, I had a whole list of flaws that were unacceptable to me in a man. At last count, I think Rob possessed every one of them! But when he gets that little twinkle in his eye he makes me feel like a princess, and the miracle happens. Instead of seeing his flaws, I can only see the goodness of his heart."

Visit Cara (and the horses, cat and Rob) at her Web site, www.Cara-Colter.com

**Harlequin Romance® presents
a beautiful love story from**

Cara Colter

**Her intense romances and engaging
characters will captivate you!**

Look out for more of Cara's books,
coming soon from Harlequin Romance®,
where you'll find stories
from the heart, for the heart!

PROLOGUE

"OH, DEAR," Mrs. Abigail Smith stammered, "Oh dear, indeed."

Mrs. Abigail Smith was not a woman easily ruffled. For forty-three years the graduates of Mrs. Smith's Academy of Fine Nannies had been eagerly sought by business moguls, financial wizards, movie stars, the old money and the nouveau riche.

Famous people did not fluster her. Au contraire! She specialized in dealing with the sometimes difficult and eccentric people of substance, and she considered it her special gift to cater to the needs of their children.

Still, for all that, Mrs. Smith had never been in the same room as a real live prince.

Prince Ryan Kaelan, House of Kaelan, Isle of Momhilegra, more commonly known as the Isle of Music, sat before her radiating *presence*.

Though she had sat across this very desk from many of the world's most powerful people, or at least their representatives, she had never quite felt this before.

Awe.

She was awed by him. He was an intimidatingly handsome

man, dressed in a long, black cashmere coat, the pristine white of a silk shirt collar showing beneath. But even without the obvious expense of those tailored clothes showing off the broadness of his shoulder, his amazing height, he would have been arresting. His physical appeal cast what Mrs. Smith's generation would have called the spell of the black Irish. He had hair the color of night, thick and manicured. The prince also possessed amazing skin, faintly copper-toned, *golden*, and his features, from high cheekbones to straight nose, to clefted chin, were unreasonably attractive.

But it was his eyes that were arresting. Midnight-blue mingled with the color of sapphires, they were ridged by sinfully sooty lashes, and they were the deep, dark eyes of a man much older than the twenty-eight years the prince had walked the earth. The prince's eyes held command, charisma…and sorrow.

"Oh dear," Mrs. Smith said again, of his request.

"Is there a problem?" His voice was the voice one would expect from a man of such stature: educated, composed, full of certainty, and yet mysterious and elusive music, the Gaelic accents of his homeland, were threaded through it. The result was, well, sensual.

Sensual? She was going to be seventy-three on her next birthday, but she felt herself blushing like a schoolgirl.

"Yes!" she said, grabbing a trifle desperately onto his own turn of phrase. "A problem! Miss Winslow is, er, otherwise engaged."

He nodded, a slight incline of his head, but his gaze locked on hers, and he tapped his leather gloves lightly against his coat sleeve, ever so faintly impatient. She felt her state of fluster grow. He was a man who expected the world to bend to his will, who was used to his every request being granted.

But Prudence Winslow for his nanny? As the royal nanny to his two motherless children, a five-year-old boy, and a baby girl, just over a year? Impossible!

"We have many nannies who are imminently suitable for this position," Mrs. Smith rushed to assure him. "In fact—" she began to go through the papers on her desk, aware that she was *pawing* in her haste to please him "—I have—"

His hand came to rest on top of hers, to stop her, and she nearly fainted at the intensity of that single, brief touch.

"I want her," he said.

Mrs. Smith felt like a fish, beached, her mouth moving, but not a sound coming out. A statement like that could be left open to wild misinterpretation!

"Her," he repeated, almost gently, gesturing to the picture in front of him, but there was no mistaking he intended to get what he wanted.

The picture he was pointing to was part of a newspaper article, the story that had put Miss P. Winslow—not to mention Mrs. Smith's Academy of Fine Nannies—on the map.

The photo looked like a heap of dark clothing collapsed in front of a car. In fact, it was Prudence Winslow, moments after she had shoved the stroller she was pushing to safety after some maniac in a stolen car had run the red light where she was crossing the street.

It had, of course, been an act of singular bravery, so far above and beyond the call of duty that the whole of New York City was proclaiming Prudence a hero. It seemed everyone now wanted nannies who were willing to place their lives on the line for their young charges.

Prudence herself, to her great credit, was annoyed by the fuss, and eager to leave the incident behind her.

And sadly, save for that one incident, Prudence was not exactly the poster child Mrs. Smith would have selected for her academy.

Prudence was simply a little *too* everything: too tall, too flamboyant and too rebellious. Too *redheaded*, Mrs. Smith thought though she knew to judge temperament by hair color was hopelessly old-fashioned. Still, that hair said it all: wild, cascading curls of pure copper, that refused to be tamed into a proper bun. And the girl's eyes: green, snapping with spunk, with spirit, with that certain mischief that made her a huge hit with children. The eyes, the hair, the height *and* the mischief added up to an unfortunate distraction to any male member of the household over the age of puberty.

Prudence's first two postings had not been great successes. *Will not wear a uniform,* the first had said as a reason for dismissal. Reading between the lines, Mrs. Smith suspected the man of the house had probably noticed Prue just a little too much. In a stroke of genius, when Prue's second posting had ended as badly as her first, Mrs. Smith had placed Prue in a single-mother home.

Still, Mrs. Smith knew she was uncharacteristically indulgent of the girl's defects, possibly because Prudence had been raised by one of her very own nannies.

When Marcus Winslow had died unexpectedly last year, it had quickly become apparent he had been holding together a house of cards. Not a penny left. And that house of cards had toppled right on top of his unsuspecting—and totally spoiled—only daughter.

Really, after the unhappy endings of those first two placements, Mrs. Smith shouldn't have given her any more chances, but she admired how Prudence had risen to the challenges tossed at her. It was very hard not to admire a person who, when handed lemons, made lemonade.

And Prudence did love children! One day, Mrs. Smith was determined, that with patience and practice, Prudence Winslow would make a fine nanny.

But to test her optimism on a prince? One that the whole world watched incessantly? Whose every tragedy, triumph— whose every breath—was so documented?

"Dear—" She blushed, realizing *dear* was not the proper form of address for a prince. "I just don't think Prudence would be a good match for your household."

"Prudence?" he said, and then smiled as if everything he had thought had been confirmed. "So, that's what the *P* stands for. A virtuous, old-fashioned name," he said, pleased, ignoring the fact *completely* that she had just told him Prudence would not do for his household.

Mrs. Smith was not sure she had ever met anyone as dramatically mismatched to her name as Prudence was! The girl had once told her she had been named after a maiden aunt in hopes of gaining her favor and fortune!

"Your Royal Highness," she said delicately, "Do you recall a movie called *The Sound of Music*?" He looked baffled, and she realized the movie was not of his generation, nor were Rodgers and Hammerstein tunes the kind of music that his kingdom, a tiny island in the southern most portion of the Irish Sea, was famous for.

The Isle of Momhilegra was known for music: classical schools, retreats for passionate music buffs, the trees that produced the most astoundingly beautiful musical instruments. At odds with its cultured reputation was its notoriety for hosting a world famous Soap Box Derby every year.

"Maria," she said helpfully, just in case, sometime, somewhere he had caught a snippet of that lovely movie. "She's more like a Maria than a Prudence."

The prince looked puzzled.

"Maria times ten," she said, a little desperately. She wanted to add, but didn't, *Maria with pizzaz. Jazz. Sex appeal.*

He'd had enough and it showed in a subtle change of his posture, the faintest hardening around the line of his mouth. He leaned forward, and pinned her with those amazing eyes.

"I would like to meet her."

The politeness of his tone did not mask the fact he had just issued poor Mrs. Smith with a royal dictate.

She told herself he had absolutely no authority anywhere in the world but his own small island nation. She told herself that, and did not for one second believe it. He was a man who carried his authority deep within him, separate from the title he enjoyed. She lowered her eyes from the devastating command of his.

"Yes, Your Highness," Mrs. Smith said.

CHAPTER ONE

PRUDENCE WINSLOW was late. And for once it wasn't her fault. Well, maybe a little her fault, but not entirely her fault.

She cast a quick look at her reflection in the doors that led her into the exquisite lobby of the Waldorf Towers, one of the grandest of the Manhattan hotels, though her father had always preferred to put up business guests in the St. Regis Club in Essex House right on the park.

She sighed at her own reflection. Disheveled. It was raining slightly, and humidity had a tendency to play havoc with hair that didn't like taming at the best of times. Coils of copper had sprung free from the bun Mrs. Smith insisted on. Mrs. Smith had also insisted on a skirt, *hem below the knee dear,* and the skirt had not stood up well to her travels, apparently disliking humidity as much as her hair.

Young Brian, clingy since the accident, and unhappy with the replacement nanny—without giving her a chance, naturally—had managed to spill butterscotch pudding on Prue's navy trench coat just as she was getting away. Despite her best—and time consuming—effort the smear had refused to be totally eradicated.

Still, she crossed the lobby with the haughtiness of a queen, and eyed the desk clerk.

Cute, she thought. Blonde. A poor girl's Brad Pitt. Then she reminded herself she was a reformed woman. Still, she had to fight the smallest urge to smile at him. Six months without so much as a date!

And six months to go, she warned herself sternly. Being as businesslike as one could be with a smear of butterscotch pudding on her lapel, *and* while fighting the temptation to just offer one little smile and see what happened, she announced, "I'm here to see, um, Kaelan Prince."

On the phone earlier, Mrs. Smith had been uncharacteristically chatty, and evasive at the same time. Prudence had gotten that a man wanted to meet her. Because of the newspaper story. Be on time, be presentable.

"A skirt," Mrs. Smith had specified sternly. "And, dear, do *something* with your hair!"

Well, she was in a skirt, not anything like the flirty little numbers she once would have worn. Mary Poppins approved. But she was not on time and not particularly presentable, either. Prue didn't want to meet a man because of all the silly attention of that newspaper story. So far, after the financial scandals surrounding her father's death, Prudence had managed to stay out of the relentless radar of the press. No connection had been made between Winslow, the-heroic-nanny, and Winslow-the-crumbled-empire.

She wanted it to stay that way, so she had tried to refuse this meeting, but Mrs. Smith had been adamant.

"For the good of the Academy, dear," she'd said.

Prue had not needed to be reminded how much she owed Mrs. Smith, who had been there for her when so few others had been.

"Kaelan Prince," she repeated to the clerk, who was looking baffled.

Suddenly a light came on for him. "Kaelan Prince? I think you must mean Prince Ryan Kaelan."

"Whatever," she said, thinking *right, everyone's a rock star,* and glancing at her watch. Ten minutes late. Shoot.

"Ah," he said, a trifle uncomfortably, "the young women over there are trying to catch a glimpse of him, as well."

Prue followed his gaze and frowned. A gaggle of young girls and women were clustered together by the elevators, giggling.

"I'm expected," she said, and saw that her change of tone affected him as much as the words. Oh, she could still be her father's daughter when she wanted to be.

"Your name, madam?" he said, picking up the phone.

She gave it to him, and he made a call. He looked at her with an entirely different kind of interest when he set down the phone. "Someone will be down to escort you immediately, Miss Winslow."

"Thank you."

Down to escort her? What was going on? Was the man really a rock star? It would be totally unlike Mrs. Smith to be influenced by celebrity.

The doors to the elevator slid open, and the small crowd by it pushed forward hopefully, and then started calling out questions. "Will he be down today? How is Gavin?" One girl, lovely, stood out from the rest. She looked all of twelve, and was wildly waving a sign that said Someday My Prince Will Come.

The child reminded Prudence of herself at twelve, hoping, craving, living in a fantasy because real life was too lonely.

Girl, she thought, *we need to talk.*

But her focus changed to an older, very dignified looking

man in a dark green uniform with gold epithets on the shoulders coming toward her. There was some sort of crest on his breast: it looked like a dragon coiled around an instrument she thought might have been a lute.

He ignored the gathering, came to her and inclined his head ever so slightly. "Miss Winslow? If you'll come with me. Ignore them," he suggested out of the side of his mouth as they passed through the throng.

"Ronald," he introduced himself as the elevator doors whispered closed, and she found herself alone with him in the elevator. She regarded him thoughtfully.

Older, but very handsome. One little smile. She sighed at how very hard it was to become a new person.

"Have you been briefed in protocol?"

"Excuse me?"

"Aside from punctuality, certain forms are expected of visitors."

He managed to say that in a way that took the sting out of the fact that he was mildly reprimanding her for being late.

"A curtsy is no longer necessary, though of course, if you desire—"

"You're kidding me, right? A curtsy?" She laughed, and then registered the faintly offended dignity on Ronald's face. She recalled, the desk clerk correcting her on the name. Not a rock star after all!

"Are you telling me," she said slowly and softly, "I'm going to meet a prince? A real prince?"

"Yes, miss. I'm sorry. I thought you knew."

Why hadn't Mrs. Smith told her this? Or had that snippet of information been buried somewhere in that muddled phone call?

No, no, NO! Life was too unfair. Coincidence was too cruel. Just like that girl at the elevator, Prudence had believed in princes. Oh, had she ever! She was the love junkie! She had collected books and movies, she had craved the things they promised. Since she was fourteen years old, and had discovered how much men liked her, she had been searching, she had *known* deep in her heart that when she kissed the right one her fairy tale would begin.

But so far she had kissed a thousand toads, and not one of them had turned into a prince.

And then, last year, after the death of her father, she had realized, ever so painfully it was the love of that remote and disconnected man that she had craved, and that now she would never receive it. Never.

She had turned over a new leaf. No romance for a year. Not a single date, not a kiss, nothing. Somewhere, she knew, in that desperate search for a prince, she had lost herself.

And lately, she'd begun to have a sense of finding what had been lost.

The universe was testing her resolve! That's what was happening. Prudence became very aware that she did not want to meet a prince, she was not ready to have her resolve tested! She eyed the emergency stop button on the elevator.

A hand touched her sleeve, and she looked into her escort's eyes. They were kind and good-humored. "There's nothing to be afraid of," he said quietly.

"Afraid?" she said defensively. She, Prudence Winslow had never been afraid of anything! Unless winding up alone counted!

And lately even thought didn't fill her with panic the way it once had. She thought, resolutely, of her volunteer work. Before finding Mrs. Smith's academy, shortly after her father's death, she had found herself at a food bank, humiliated and hungry. Now, every spare moment and cent she had were spent paying back to that wonderful organization that not only fed the hungry, but allowed them to keep their dignity.

Her life was on track! She wasn't ready for this challenge. She just wasn't.

"Dammit," she said, and tried to capture some of those loose curls and force them back into place.

Her escort eyed her with a trace of uneasiness. "Naturally we don't curse in the presence of His Royal Highness," he said, tactfully.

"Naturally," she repeated, gave up on her hair and folded her restless hands primly in front of her.

"The correct form of address, when you are presented to him, is Your Royal Highness, not Prince Ryan. After the initial meeting, you may call him 'sir.'"

"Ah," she said. "But no curtsy."

If he detected even a hint of sarcasm, he pretended not to. "Unless you want to," he assured her.

"Believe me, I don't." An attempt at a curtsy would probably land her right on her nose not, thank heaven, that she was the curtsying type. Even in her fantasies!

Ronald's sigh was barely audible. "I believe you." The elevator doors slid open and she was led across a thickly carpeted hallway to double doors that opened to sheer opulence.

The hotel suite was resplendent with vases of fresh, sweet-scented lilies. There was a grand piano in the main room, silk-covered sofas, rich carpeting. An elegant chandelier dripped raindrops of light, the fireplace was lit against the dampness of the day.

"May I take your coat?"

She didn't want to surrender her coat, even with its stain! It felt like some form of protection!

Against what? she asked herself annoyed. She shrugged off the stained jacket. Underneath she had on a plain white blouse that had been pressed, but was intent on reacting to the humidity in the same way as the skirt and her hair.

"Please, have a seat," Ronald said. "I will announce you."

But she couldn't sit. She studied the tasteful paintings, the view out the window, glanced in at the dining room that was through adjoining double doors. A maid, in a crisp uniform, was setting the Queen Anne table for eight.

The time ticked by. Why was she here? Why had Mrs. Smith sent her here? Prudence hated this! She did not like mysteries. Since her father's death she was absolutely allergic to surprises. She liked control, the neat and tidy little world that she was building for herself, the amount of money she was managing to raise for Loaves and Fishes.

Once upon a time, that amount of money would have seemed laughable to her.

It occurred to her, she did not want to be using the phrase *once upon a time* when she was about to meet a prince. She was the girl who had sworn off fairy tales! Suddenly she relaxed. She got it! The prince was going to be ugly. Old. Fat. Balding. She was here to learn how ridiculous her fantasies had always been!

The universe wasn't testing her. It was rewarding her, saying, *girl, you are on the right track.*

Just in case she was wrong, she eyed the door wistfully, but knew she could not let Mrs. Smith down. If Mrs. Smith wanted her to meet a prince, and thought it might be in some way good for Mrs. Smith's Academy of Fine Nannies, Prudence would do her best.

Did Mrs. Smith know, that if you said it really fast, three times in a row, the last time it came out Mrs. Smith's Academy of Nine Fannies? What if Prue accidentally said that to the prince? What if she *thought* about it when she was with him? At her father's funeral, she had suddenly thought of the time she had wrapped his favorite dog, Kelpie, in toilet paper, and then she'd had to fight the absurd desire to giggle for the rest of the service.

This was going to be the same. She just knew it. She might as well leave now, before she brought eternal shame down on the Academy of Nine Fannies.

But before she could act, the double doors opened on the other side of the suite, and Ronald came through first, holding the door.

Prue felt her mouth fall open at the man who swept through those open doors, and she snapped it shut.

He was not ugly. Old. Fat. Balding. He was every girl's fantasy of what a prince should be. If ever a story started *once upon a time*, it would be the story that began with him sweeping into the room.

Mrs. Smith's Academy of Nine Fannies was wiped from her mind as she watched the man cross the room toward her.

He was tall enough to make her feel small, and at five feet eleven inches Prue had not enjoyed that sensation since she was about eight years old. He was dressed in an ivory sweater, dark shirt and dark slacks, but even if he had been dressed in dungarees there would have been no mistaking his station in life. He carried himself with a kind of pure confidence, the inborn grace of a man who knew exactly who he was. He carried himself as a man born to inherit the very earth, and he knew it.

Though each of his features was chiseled masculine perfection, it was his eyes that caught and held her. They were an astounding shade of blue, reminding her of the waters off the Hawaiian coast of Kona, where her father had kept a winter house.

Still, she told herself desperately, he was not at all her type. She had decided long ago that a man with dark coloring wouldn't do. If she married someone fair, her children might be strawberry-blondes, instead of flaming redheads!

Plus, something about his confidence set her teeth on edge, because it looked like it bordered on arrogance, and arrogance headed her list of fatal flaws that barred a man from ever being her Mr. Right. Of course, the list contained many other items, terribly superficial, but important to her nonetheless, from hairy nostrils to bad toenails!

The prince was the one who closed the space between them, since she found she could not move. He extended his hand, which she had not expected. She shot a look at Ronald, and caught his slight nod. She took the hand offered her.

And felt enormous strength…and something else, a sizzle of pure awareness, despite his dark coloring and the fact she had not inspected his toenails, though his nostrils were a definite pass. Still, the feeling was not appropriate—not nanny and prince, but man and woman.

The universe was being exceedingly cruel! She jerked her hand out of his. There was no feeling in the world she had to fight more than that one! Oh, how that *feeling* could make a woman weak, and cloud her judgment.

She should know.

No, there was no trusting yourself once that *zing,* was in the air, once that *hope* blossomed to life. In no time at all, she would be wasting hours of her life mooning, shopping for the perfect little *thinking-of-you* card, waiting for the phone to ring, trying on dresses with a view to what *he* might like.

She was having this reaction without his passing the toenail test!

It felt as if every bit of progress she had made in the last six months was suddenly threatened by a single touch from this stranger. It was as if the bottom was falling out of her world, as if she was tumbling crazily down with it.

"Miss Winslow," he said, and his voice was an enchantment—deep, masculine, faintly musical. "What a pleasure."

She *loved* his accent. She tried to bite out *Your Royal Highness,* but somehow she could not. If she knew how to curtsy, she suspected she would!

She tried to tuck a wayward curl behind her ear, failed, and then shoved her hands behind her back.

Say something, she ordered herself. "Hi."

She felt the man in the green uniform's tiny flinch, but if the prince was in any way offended it did not show.

He regarded her with those clear, astonishing eyes, and then smiled faintly.

The smile was devastating, despite the fact his two front teeth were faintly crooked and over lapped each other. Crooked teeth was on her list!

Still, that smile took the faint sternness on a face too young to hold sternness and washed it away. The faint imperfection of his teeth was oddly *appealing*.

So, despite the teeth his mouth was entirely kissable. One kiss and she would know. Prince, or toad?

Stop it, she ordered herself.

"Please," he said, "have a seat." He gestured to a chair, and then took a seat on the sofa at right angles to it. "Would you care for a refreshment?"

Whiskey on the rocks. Make it a double. "No, thank you." She knew she should add Your Royal Highness or at least sir, but she was unable to do so, barely able to squeak out her refusal.

"Tell me a little about yourself," he invited.

She stared at him, and then asked, flabbergasted, "Why?"

He frowned slightly. She suspected he was not accustomed to any request being questioned. Arrogant, she reminded herself. Still, he regarded her so thoughtfully she had to fight to keep from squirming.

Finally he said, "I read about your act of heroism in the newspaper. I'm here in New York on business. It made me curious about you."

"Oh." There was a terrible desire to spill it all—about the fear and loneliness and crippling self-doubt and self-evaluation and humiliation since her father's death. There was a terrible desire to dismiss the arrogance, and trust whatever it was she saw in those eyes.

Depth?

Those eyes, she reminded herself, that had complete strangers in the lobby making fools of themselves, waving signs that said Someday My Prince Will Come.

"There's nothing to know," she said, hastily, her voice cool in defense of that familiar craving that she *felt*.

His silence was as commanding as his question had been, so she added, "Really."

He still said nothing, and so she felt compelled to fill the silence between them.

"It wasn't an act of heroism," she said hurriedly, though

she realized probably one did not *correct* the prince. "It wasn't anything of the sort. It happened very quickly, and I never once made a conscious decision. I was crossing the street with the light, I realized a car was coming much too quickly, and that it wasn't going to stop. I managed to shove the stroller out of the way, the car hit me. Not even very hard, really."

She had a bruise on her hip the size of a pineapple, but even *thinking* about her naked hip in the presence of the prince seemed wildly off color, like thinking of nine fannies, which of course now she was!

"But isn't that the nature of true courage?" he asked softly, "That it comes naturally, without a conscious thought?"

"No," she said, "it's not. True courage is to feel fear, and then to act in an honorable way, despite that."

"Is it possible both forms are equally relevant?"

She had a feeling of being in a dream. She, who was only an hour removed from having butterscotch pudding spilled down her front, she who had irreverent and uncontrollable thoughts about the name of her employer's most dignified business, she who thought about toilet paper wrapped dogs at funerals, was now sitting in a suite having a philosophical conversation with a prince. She was trying desperately to see him through the filter of her Fatal Flaws List, and just as desperately trying to conduct herself with some semblance of grace.

Prudence might have laughed at the absurdity of life, if she didn't make the mistake of meeting his eyes.

She saw it again. Depth. Something absurdly compelling. Eyes like that could make a woman do or say something really stupid.

Mrs. Smith's Academy of Nine Fannies.

"It wasn't courage," she insisted. "Instinct."

"A mother having that kind of instinct I could understand. But to put yourself in such peril for a child that was not your own, that is something else."

"I'm trying to tell you it was nothing," she said.

"And I'm trying to tell you," he said, his voice soft with command, "that it was something."

"Oh." Nearly as bad as *hi* but the man was stealing her breath and her wits at the same time as he was being arrogant! He hadn't even been there. Who was he to decide what it had or hadn't been?

"I am considering offering you a position in my household."

She stared at him, aghast. She was barely going to be able to survive this interview with her vow intact. No men. No kisses. No attractions. No dates. No. No. No. She had six months to go! He was flawed, obviously, but to test herself by working in his household? Never!

"Your Royal Prince," she said, "I don't want to work for you. I mean in your household. I mean I am very happy where I'm at."

Your Royal Prince! Mrs. Smith should have never trusted her with this kind of delicate assignment!

She didn't like that smile one little bit, now. It said clearly that what she wanted was of little or no significance to him.

His life was about getting what he wanted. She suspected always. She *hated* that. Men who always get what they want was moving to number one on her list.

"I look after children," she stated uneasily. "What would I do in your household?"

"I have two children," he answered.

For some reason that left her flummoxed. She hadn't thought he was married. Why not? How couldn't he be? When he looked like that, and obviously the female population was intent on throwing themselves at him, how could he be unattached?

Oh, so this was what the universe was showing her. The prince was not ugly, fat, old or bald, though he did have some flaws. The biggest one: yippee, he was unavailable. She should be dancing for joy! Instead she felt strangely bereft, already giving in to her former self!

"I'm a widower," he said softly.

She did not like the stab of sympathy that flashed through her. Or the strange sensation of relief. So, he was available. He was definitely not available to the likes of her.

Not that she was in the market for a prince. Not now.

"I don't want to change jobs," she said, a little more desperately. What she meant was she did not want to work for *him*. She did not want to indulge that small, weak part of her that wanted to believe in fairy tales!

And she truly did not want to change jobs. She loved little Brian. In that very instant she forgave him the butterscotch stain on her best coat. Besides, Loaves and Fishes needed her! She was proving an inspired fund-raiser.

A door opened behind them, and her green clad escort came in. And through the open door with him, unnoticed save by her, slipped a child.

He was a devilish looking little imp, perhaps five. He tucked himself behind the back of the sofa the prince was seated on. Ronald bent and said something to the prince in an undertone, the prince turned his attention over his shoulder to him.

Prue watched the place where the small boy was. Sure enough, in a moment, the unruly black hair appeared over the sofa, and then eyes bright and blue and full of dark mischief. The child's eyebrows beetled down as he regarded her with pint-size disapproval. There was no doubting he was his father's son!

She beetled hers back at him.

He shifted upward, so that his face was revealed. He was an exceptionally handsome little boy. He regarded her with what she could only conclude was patent dislike—much like Brian had shown the temporary nanny this morning. Then he crossed his eyes and stuck out his tongue, not in play.

She shot a look at the prince, who was still otherwise engaged, and then looked back at the child.

She did something that probably would have given Mrs. Smith a heart attack. Prudence crossed her eyes and stuck out her tongue back.

Ryan chose that moment to look back at her.

He had to bite the side of his cheek to keep from reacting to her crossed eyes and her tongue stuck out. He felt as if he had been biting the side of his cheek since the moment he had first seen her.

The truth was nothing—not his meeting with Mrs. Smith, and not the photo in the paper—had prepared him for Miss Prudence Winslow in the flesh.

She was tall and slender, and had one of the most magnificent heads of hair he had ever seen. Those red curls crackled and curled around her head as if they were filled with electricity. She was intensely beautiful—a perfect nose, wide mouth, milky skin—not at all the demure nanny Mrs. Smith's rather plain office and the heap of clothes in the newspaper picture had led him to believe he would be meeting.

Her eyes were as green as the pool beneath Myria Falls, on his island home, and they flashed with spirit, a subtle defiance, again on a collision course with his expectations.

Though her clothes were rumpled and dowdy, she carried herself with such cache that it looked as if the clothes were meant to be that way!

She was really the kind of woman a man should be prepared to meet, and he was not.

The defiance showed itself again when she did not use his title, and when she did, she used it incorrectly. Deliberately?

She had been tardy and rude, and though he suspected neither was intentional, he was aware within moments of meeting her that she would not be a good fit in his smoothly run household, just as Mrs. Smith had tried to warn him.

The people retained by his family had worked those positions through generations, father teaching son, mother teaching daughter. They were proud to be of service to the House of Kaelan. A woman like this one would be a terrible disruption to the routine of the castle, which had probably not changed in three hundred years.

The thought made him feel oddly restless, rather than contented.

Besides, the royal nannies were proving problematic. It was a different age than the one he had been raised in, and the prince was aware of wanting something—no, aching for something—different for his children. His son in particular was having such problems since the death of his mother. The child who had always been like the sun was querulous now, and angry. His mischief ran to meanness.

His son, Gavin, needed someone not quite so rigid as the nanny Ryan had just dismissed a week ago. He needed something. He was not sure what, but when he saw Prudence Winslow he was certain she was it.

And when he turned back from his conversation with Ronald, to see her green eyes crossed and her tongue out, he thought for the first time, *I've made a mistake. My instincts were wrong. Let her go back to her life.*

But then, surprised, he became aware his son had arrived in the room and tucked himself behind the sofa. He turned and gave Gavin a look he intended to be stern, but the look melted.

Gavin was smiling.

And not that wicked black smile that Ryan had come to dread, that meant his son had been up to no good, had been tormenting the staff, or the baby, or his nanny, or one of the queen's dogs. Six nannies in six months because of one small, hurting child.

No, on Gavin's face was a true smile, tentative, but true. When he saw his father watching him, the smile disappeared, he glared and marched from the room.

"That was my son, Gavin," Ryan said, watching her face. "He lost his mother thirteen months ago. He's having a hard time of it."

He saw, finally, what he needed to see in her eyes. Not pride and not belligerence, a terrible softness, so soft he could feel a longing in himself.

He killed it quickly. His entire marriage he had *longed.* He had been young and hoped for happiness, despite the fact the marriage had been arranged. Raina had hoped, too. She had hoped by marrying so well, by marrying a prince, by becoming a princess, she could forget that she had loved another....

Sternly he turned his thoughts from those painful memories. He had two beautiful children.

"There's a baby as well," he said, watching her even more closely. For some reason, he found himself fishing in the pocket underneath his sweater, passing her the photo of his little Sara. "She's still a little too young to travel with me."

Prudence hesitated, then leaned forward and took the photo.

The tiniest of smiles tickled her lips.

Sara had that effect on people: with her sparse hair always standing straight up, black dandelion fluff, and her huge eyes, blue, intense, curious.

"She's thirteen months old. My wife died while giving birth to her."

"I'm so sorry," she said, and she meant it. Her eyes drifted from the picture, followed where Gavin had gone.

Ryan felt something in him sigh with relief. She would love his children. That was the ingredient that made you guard someone else's child with your own life.

Love.

The missing ingredient in his life. The thought was renegade and he amended it quickly, the missing ingredient in all the other nannies, including the ones he had grown up with.

Caring, of course. Dedicated, yes. Respectful, naturally.

But always falling just a hair short of what he saw, unguarded, for just a moment in the green of Prudence Winslow's eyes as she looked at the place where his son had stood only moments ago.

He had managed to get some skimpy paperwork on the nanny from Mrs. Smith. He knew Prudence Winslow was qualified for this job.

But where he really knew it, that place he had learned to count on more than any other, his instinct. Instinct had told him not to marry Raina. But he'd been twenty-two, under pressure, not really given a choice…

Since then, aware of the cataclysmic consequences of ignoring his instincts, Ryan tried to pay more attention to that voice. It had been nagging him since he had first seen the picture, and now it whispered, firmly, *yes*.

Even though she would probably never call him Your Royal Highness without nearly choking, even though his household was probably not ready for her, and neither was he, he knew his children needed her. He had known that from the moment he had seen that newspaper and read about a young nanny who had put the life of her young charge ahead of her own.

"I want you to think about returning to the Isle of Momhilegra with me," he said. "As the head—" Suddenly he was no more able to call her a nanny, than she was able to call him Your Royal Highness. "To look after my children," he amended.

She stared at him, looked away, leaped suddenly to her feet.

"May I have my coat?" Her cheeks were staining a beautiful, angry shade of red. "Thank you, but I said no. I'm very happy with the position I have now."

For a moment her eyes trailed to his lips, the look in them so intense he felt scorched. But then her coat was brought and she left in a flurry of activity.

He smiled slightly as the door slammed behind her. "Ronald?"

"Yes, sir?"

"I'd like to watch a movie this afternoon. *The Sound of Music*. Could you find it for me?"

"Certainly, sir."

"And there's something else I need done."

Ronald listened to his request, nodded his head. By later today, if things were as he hoped, Miss Winslow was going to find herself dismissed from her current position.

Other men might have worried about such a high-handed approach to another's life, but Ryan was a man of complete discipline, who had known only one reality his entire life, and that reality was that duty came before personal dreams, personal desires.

Of course, in terms of his marriage that had been disastrous, but he wasn't, after all, marrying Miss Winslow. He was employing her. It did not really occur to him that Miss Winslow might resent his decision-making on her behalf. People liked working for him. They were compensated beyond their wildest dreams. Her initial reluctance to accept his offer would most certainly turn to gratitude, if she was a reasonable woman.

So, with that taken care of Ryan, settled in to watch the movie. He invited Gavin to watch it with him, but his son wanted to play a video game on the television in his bedroom. *And not be in the same room as his father.*

The movie was entertaining, a good diversion from his frustration over yet another rejection by Gavin. Still, when he turned the movie off, Ryan felt pensive despite the "feel-good" theme of the show.

Maria times ten? That did not add up to a reasonable woman. Plus, Maria would have never looked at a man's lips in a way that would leave him feeling scorched!

"Oh, dear," he said borrowing a phrase from Mrs. Smith. "Oh dear, indeed."

CHAPTER TWO

"YOU'RE firing me?" Prudence asked, stunned.

Mrs. Hilroy knitted her hands together, and looked around Prue's humble basement quarters with discomfort.

"Of course I'm not *firing* you," she stammered uneasily. "There must be a way to say this that is gentle and expresses what you mean to me. And Brian. Terminated. No, no, that's much too harsh. I'm letting you go. Yes! Letting you go. To brighter things. And bigger things."

Prudence knew, hollowly, that no matter how frantically Mrs. Hilroy tried to sugarcoat her announcement, it was all semantics. She was being dismissed. This morning she had a job. Now she did not. How could she not have seen this coming?

"You saved Brian's life," Mrs. Hilroy gushed.

How good of you to remember that, Prue thought sadly. "I think this is the worst day of my life."

"Surely you exaggerate," Mrs. Hilroy said with dismay.

"Probably," Prudence agreed dryly. Worst day was possibly too dramatic. The day her father had died had been worse. The weeks following had been one terrible day after another. Not just because of his staggering financial disasters, but because she'd had to realize the love a small, lost, lonely child had craved from him was never going to happen. She'd had to grow up.

But today had been a horrendous day, even if it did not rate as highly on the horrible scale as did others. She was losing her position with the Hilroys!

Ever since her interview with the prince, Prue had a sense, not exactly of foreboding, but of her world being shaken, tested. Her sense of herself had felt wobbly and strained ever since she had first looked into the amazing blue of his eyes, listened to the masculine melody of his speech. In some language, unspoken, he had asked her to look at herself differently.

When she damn well didn't want to! She didn't want to ask herself questions like, was she truly happy or did loneliness yap at her heels like a small dog protecting its yard? She didn't want to ask herself what did her future hold? Where was her life going?

She especially did not want to ask herself if her Fatal Flaws List was, well, flawed. It was retired anyway!

She was glad she had told him no. It probably rated as one of the better decisions of her life! She felt as if the devil had met her and held out what she most wanted. Despite the fact Prince Kaelan had some flaws that didn't fit the picture, it was still the fairy-tale fantasy and she'd developed the strength of character in the last few months to recognize it for exactly what it was!

A lie. An illusion.

No prince was coming to rescue her. She was on her own!

And now, after hearing Mrs. Hilroy's announcement, she was really on her own. Out-on-her-ear on her own!

She felt the smallest tinge of regret about her interview

with the prince. If she'd heard him out, she might have found out if he was paying more than the pittance she made here!

Used to make here.

Certainly whatever accommodations he was offering had to be better than this cold, barely finished room, tucked in between the noisy furnace and the laundry room in the Hilroys's basement.

The thought of going back to him now, hat in hand, saying she was suddenly available was just too humiliating. Besides, she could not work for a man with eyes like that!

But on the other hand she was certain if she lost another position, Miss Smith was going to wash her hands of her, heroics not withstanding. This was her third chance, her "bus ride" as she told Brian when they were playing Go Fish and he had run out of toothpicks to bet! Mrs. Smith had been tolerant, and remarkably supportive, but Prudence had always been aware that this posting with the Hilroys had been her last chance with the Academy of Fine Nannies.

"It's just that since the accident," Mrs. Hilroy said, "I'm so aware of wanting to be with my son. Of *needing* to be with him. What if you hadn't thrown him clear that day? What if I would have missed the last day of his life? Traded moments with him for money?"

Prue gathered her wits and looked at Mrs. Hilroy's distraught face. Her self-pity was replaced with reluctant compassion. If Brian was her son, she wouldn't want to leave him to go to work every day. Mrs. Hilroy was making the right decision, the noble decision, a decision that put Brian's needs first.

My work here is done, Prudence thought, but could not completely bite back a sigh. "So, it has nothing to do with me, then? It's not because of my performance?"

"Prudence, you have been a breath of fresh air in this house. My child adores you. But, selfishly, I want him to cry and fuss when I leave to go out, not when you do."

A perfectly reasonable way for a mother to feel.

"When do you need me to vacate my room?" Prue asked, dully. "I don't suppose you'll be needing a cleaning lady, will you?"

It hurt to say that. It was humbling to say that. And completely unnecessary. There had to be thousands of jobs she was well qualified to do. But it gave her a headache to think about it. And she needed to be employed again *fast*. She had no savings, and no health care, and despite her love of Loaves and Fishes, she had rather hoped never to need their services again!

She felt like a disgrace and a loser, and it was humbling how fast she could feel that way when she had been working so hard to make her self-esteem become about her, become so much more than the man on her arm.

"B-b-but, I understood you had been offered another job," Mrs. Hilroy wailed.

The budding compassion Prue had been feeling for her employer left her with a plop that was almost audible in the tight confines of her small room. Understanding curled in her like sour milk hitting hot coffee.

Even as she warned herself to keep her legendary temper, Prudence stalked over to Mrs. Hilroy who took a step back from her.

"Excuse me?" Prue said dangerously.

"I understood you had been offered a job. Prudence, by a prince! Are you mad? How could you refuse an opportunity like that?"

"How do you know about that?" Prue asked softly.

Mrs. Hilroy went very quiet. Her eyes slid away from Prue's.

"Who told you I'd been offered another job? Mrs. Smith?"

"Actually I talked to Abigail first, but I was very upset. I didn't want to let you go! And then he called himself."

Himself. In an outrageous tone of voice that should be reserved for the pope or the president. Okay, or maybe a prince. "You spoke to him?"

"Just on the phone," Mrs. Hilroy said. "I've never spoken to a prince before. It was lovely."

Prudence stared hard at her employer. Ex-employer. Mrs. Hilroy had the same expression on her face as those ridiculous females that had waited outside the elevator at the Waldorf.

"He seemed like a very nice man," Mrs. Hilroy said, just a hint of defiance in her soft, wavering voice.

Oh! Never mind that Prue had questioned the wisdom of dismissing his offer without further investigation, had been raking herself over the coals for the way she had handled her interview with the prince, and her exit from it!

Never mind that! This was her life, and she was not having it wrested from her control by some high and mighty mucky-muck who was accustomed to buying whatever and whomever he wanted.

She decided, that very second, that arrogance topped the Fatal Flaws List for future employers as well as future husbands!

Prue studied Mrs. Hilroy, who was steadily crumpling under the sternness of her gaze. She knew the truth. "He paid you! To get rid of me!"

Mrs. Hilroy's eyes were doing the evasive slide, again. "He

offered me, er, compensation. So I could afford to stay home with Brian."

"That's evil! He played to your weakest point, your love of your child!"

"It wasn't like that! He was *nice*."

"He's the devil," Prudence decided. "Do you think the devil looks like a monster, and comes hurtling frightening curses? Oh, no, he comes in a guise, a prince no less, and holds out what tempts you most. Of course he's *nice*."

Mrs. Hilroy looked baffled. She said firmly, "Prudence, you are no kind of expert on demons."

Ah, perhaps not, though she felt as if she had been wrestling her own for so long it was exhausting.

"You sold me to him for silver," she accused Mrs. Hilroy.

"People can't sell other people," Mrs. Hilroy said, but there was a measure of doubt in her voice.

"Well, he's about to find that out!"

"Prudence, don't be rash! Please. This is an opportunity. You need to think about it carefully."

A part of her knew that was true. A part of her knew she was being given a rare second chance to handle things differently than she had the first time. A part of her knew that Prince Ryan Kaelan was not the devil, that the devils she fought were within herself.

But he was a man who could hurt her like no other ever had if she let down the guard she had built up around herself, the fortress around her heart.

Besides there was a part of her—a handicap since birth— that was not the least bit interested in being rational and calm, that insisted on acting on the glory of impulse, even if there was a price to be paid for that later.

"I already have thought about it," she snapped.

In the far reaches of the house, they heard a doorbell ring.

Mrs. Hilroy blushed. "That might be him. He said he would come to call at nine. Imagine that. Do you think cookies will be all right?"

"Cookies? Mrs. Hilroy, you do not sit the devil down in your front parlor and feed him cookies! I can't believe he would come here. The audacity of the man! What am I supposed to do? Meekly pack my bag and allow myself to be carried away to some kingdom on the other end of the earth?"

"It's not really. Momhilegra is between England and Ireland, in the Irish Sea."

"You discussed it with him?" Prue asked, incensed. How long had Mrs. Hilroy and the prince had their cozy little chat? What secrets did he know about her that she would much rather he didn't know? Secrets people learned when they lived together. Secrets that should be sacred, like that sometimes when Brian wrapped chubby arms around her neck and kissed her cheek, she cried.

Mrs. Hilroy's blush deepened. "No, of course not. I discussed nothing with him. Our conversation was extremely brief."

Prue's relief that he knew none of her secrets was out of proportion to the fact she was about to dismiss Prince Ryan Kaelan from her life, permanently.

And it was going to feel good! Dismissing the prince, high-handed, arrogant ass that he was. Really, what she would be doing was dismissing her own temptations!

"I just had a little peek at the atlas. After I'd hung up."

The doorbell chimed again.

"I don't think it's good manners to keep a prince waiting," Mrs. Hilroy said.

"Good manners! What has he done to deserve good manners? He's had me dismissed from my job! Do you think what he's doing is a show of decorum? Or respect for other people?"

"I think you are taking this entirely the wrong way," Mrs. Hilroy said, with surprising firmness, straightening her spine, and meeting Prue's eyes dead-on for the first time since she had come into the basement. "He wants you to be a nanny to his motherless children. It's not as if he's spiriting you off to join his harem."

Mrs. Hilroy blushed. So did Prudence. That rather erotic thought hung in the air for a moment, and before Prudence melted under the heat of it, she shook herself free, gave Mrs. Hilroy one last look and bounded up the stairs.

She marched through the house and had built up a good head of steam by the time she flung open the front door.

Poor Ronald stood there looking like a drowned rat, the rain pouring down around him, his gold epithets withered like wet paper on his shoulders.

"Good to see you again, miss," he said, and smiled with charming sincerity.

Darn, she liked Ronald. He was just doing his job. But now was no time for weakness. "Tell His Royal High-handedness no!" she said and slammed the door.

A moment passed. The doorbell rang again.

She opened it, and Ronald stood there doing his best to look dignified. She folded her arms over her chest, and tapped her foot. "No," she said. "As in I am not coming to work for him, not now, not next week, not ever, not if it was the last position on the face of the earth, not if I was starving in a hovel, not if—"

"That's rather a lot for me to remember, miss. Perhaps you could tell him yourself. He's in the car."

She looked over Ronald's shoulder to the long, black limo that was parked, purring, across the street. The windows were darkly tinted.

"He's destroyed my life, and I'm supposed to go stand in the rain, tap humbly on the window of his car, wait until he opens it and then offer a suitable explanation as to why I do not want my life arranged by him? Perhaps it would be a nice touch if I were to beg his forgiveness for inconveniencing him by wanting to run my own life?"

Ronald looked hopeful, as if she might be getting the idea.

"Tell him to—to go to the blazes!" She wished she could have thought of something much stronger, but it was spur of the moment. She made up for her lack of imagination by slamming the door extra hard, but it didn't close before she saw the look of trepidation on Ronald's face.

Apparently no one had ever told good Prince Ryan to go to the blazes before.

Well, in that case it would do him nothing but good. Prudence could not help but feel it was about time someone did!

She peeked out the curtain and watched Ronald make his lonely way across the street. His shoulders were hunched against the rain.

She felt a little sorry for him. She hoped the prince would not shoot the messenger. She let the curtain drop and savored the pride she felt in herself.

Temptation had not just knocked. Oh, no. It had tried to grab her by the throat! And she had still managed to send it packing.

"You are a different girl than you were six months ago," she told herself proudly.

* * *

Ryan watched Ronald cross the street, alone. Ronald slid into the driver's seat, brushed rain from his shoulders and after a very long moment met Ryan's eye in the mirror.

"Is she just getting her suitcase then?" Ryan asked.

"Ah, no sir. I don't believe she's coming."

Ryan contemplated that. He had made all the arrangements with Mrs. Smith this afternoon, he had looked after Prudence Winslow's current position. Not coming?

"Did she say why?"

"Not exactly, sir."

"What *exactly* did she say?"

Ronald hesitated long enough that Ryan knew this wasn't unfolding smoothly in accordance with his plan, or the way he always ran his life, personal and business.

He felt a tinge of impatience, and resentment. He'd come out personally, on such a dismal night, to welcome her to his employ!

"She said to tell you to go to the blazes."

"Excuse me?"

Even though they both knew he had heard it perfectly the first time, Ronald helpfully repeated it. And added, "And she said she couldn't be bothered getting herself wet to come and tell you personally."

Ryan contemplated what he was feeling.

Never, in his entire life, had anyone ever said anything even remotely like that to him. His relationship with his wife had not been good, but she had never spoken a harsh word to him. No, she had killed him slowly, with politeness, by looking straight at him, and never seeing him.

He tried to feel indignant about this introduction to this

world of—would squabbling be the right word—but found he did not.

What he felt was strangely curious, dangerously intrigued.

He opened the car door. "I guess we should give the lady a chance to say what she needs to say to me, *personally.*"

"A terrible idea, if I've ever heard one, sir," Ronald offered, with a slow shake of his head. But he was smiling slightly, and with strange indulgence.

Ryan crossed the street in long strides. He saw the front window curtain flick back, and was unsurprised that the little minx was watching him with pleasure. It was absolutely pouring, and he was soaked by the time he got to the door. He had to ring the bell three times before it was answered, even though he knew damn well she was standing right behind it.

And then it squeaked open, and she was standing there, bristling with angry energy, not the least contrite that she had kept him waiting in the downpour.

And he still didn't feel indignant. In fact, he hoped he wasn't gawking.

Prudence Winslow looked absolutely magnificent. Gone was the bun and the dowdy nanny outfit he had been treated to this afternoon.

Her hair was down, falling in a wave of crackling, wildfire past the curve of her slender shoulders.

She was wearing a shimmering camisole, the thin straps not looking like they were up to the job of containing the delicate swell of her heaving bosom. The daintiness of the camisole was coupled with denims that rode low on the curve of her hips and made her look leggy and slender as a young filly. Her feet were bare.

The Mrs. Smith-approved outfit she had worn earlier today had given no indication that something so wildly sensual—Bohemian even—hid in her. But her hair had hinted.

And her eyes had more than hinted, especially in that flash fire moment when they had touched on his lips. Now, her eyes were spitting sparks, like the sun striking emeralds.

Prudence Winslow was gorgeous. A complication in a nanny, of course.

"Good evening," he finally said, as if he was greeting her for the ball, as if the rain was not flowing off him in rivulets, and as if she was not standing there in a top that looked suspiciously like lingerie, in bare feet and worn jeans with her hair cascading around her as if she had just been up to something...and wonderful.

"Good evening?" she said, her voice snapping with the same electrical and passionate energy as her eyes. "Good evening? How dare you? How dare you act as though you haven't just wrecked my whole life?"

"Wrecked your life? That's ridiculous. I'm offering you a position better than the one you had here. How can that be wrecking your life?"

"You can't just do that!"

She had actually stamped her foot, to emphasize her statement, and he found himself trying very hard not to smile. Smiling right now would be a huge mistake. Huge.

"I can't?" he asked, mildly. "Why ever not?"

"Because I have to agree to it! This is America. This is not a feudal system where your lordship's eye catches on some peasant girl walking down the cobbled street with her goat on a leash and her chickens in a basket and decides he must have her."

She had branded his homeland a backward and primitive

place, and he was aware he should have felt scorned, but instead the words had the effect on him of a touch—hot, teasing, sensual—and he felt his blood turn to fire.

He felt as if, in a flash, the blood of his ancestors, warrior chieftains one and all, stirred to life within him.

The family name, Kaelan, was Gaelic for powerful in battle, and he sensed the battle this woman would give him.

A wise man would walk away, walk back to his car, shake off the rain and the memory of her with it. A wise man would return to Mrs. Smith and ask her humbly about those other nannies that she had proclaimed imminently suitable for his household.

Ryan Kaelan had been a wise man his entire life, controlled, dispassionate. He was a man who knew how to make decisions for the greater good, measured decisions, all factors weighed and balanced until one answer became crystal clear.

But now, all he could think was how he would like to wrap his hands in the red fury of her hair and pull her to him, and tame her lips with his own.

The thought shocked him so thoroughly that he took a step back from her. The slight protection of the overhang was gone, and the water sluiced over him.

He made the fatal mistake. He smiled.

"You may think this is amusing, but you can't buy me," she shouted over the rain. "I am not for sale. I told you no. And I meant it!"

"If you'd just be reasonable for a minute—"

"Reasonable?" she hissed. "Reasonable? I've just been dismissed from a job I loved because of you and you want reason?"

"Well, as a matter of fact, yes, I do."

"I'll give you reason!" She looked around, reached behind the door and came out with a crystal vase full of flowers.

Somehow he knew it was not going to be a peace offering.

She hurtled the container at his head.

He ducked easily enough, and the container shattered on the walk behind him. He turned and gazed at the wrecked flowers and broken glass, and then turned and looked back at her.

She had gone very still. "Oh," she said softly. "Look what you've made me do!" And then she slammed the door again.

He stood outside, being soaked through to the skin, and not the least perturbed by it.

Obviously he had learned things he needed to learn. She would be a terrible nanny. She would be a terrible disruption to his life and his island. She was opinionated, and had a fiery temper. Passion crackled in her eyes and in the air around her.

Still, he was aware of what he should be feeling.

Prince Ryan Kaelan, House of Kaelan, Isle of Momhilegra, had just been shouted at in a public street. Had a vase hurtled at his head!

He should be realizing the error of ever wanting her to come to his household. He should be feeling angry, or at the very least annoyed.

He had never in his life been treated like that.

And he had never in his life felt quite like this.

Alive.

Wholly, wonderfully alive, as if the rain was fire and not water, as if it was heating his skin, rather than chilling it.

He shoved his hands in his coat pocket, picked his way through the shattered glass and broken flowers and then dashed back across the street. Ronald was standing in the pouring rain with the door open, and he shut it quietly as Ryan got in the limousine.

Ronald got in his own door, looked straight ahead and pulled away in silence. Still, when they were nearly at the hotel, he finally asked in a small, incredulous voice, "Did she throw the vase at you then, sir?"

"She did," Ryan replied, and could hear the remarkable lack of offense in his voice.

He was aware, that despite the broken glass and slammed door, he had no sense of this being over.

Instead he was reviewing the whole situation like a warrior looking back over the battle, looking for the errors, the tactical mistakes, planning his next strategy.

It came to him. A man would never succeed with a woman like that by ordering her around. She would have to be wooed.

If he felt a moment's uneasiness at the use of the word *woo* in what was really a search for a nanny, he brushed it aside. He had a competitive nature. In his entire life he had never failed to get anything that he wanted.

Except, a voice insisted on whispering, *the love of your wife.*

He reminded himself that he had seen the look on Gavin's face this afternoon, though he thought he might be kidding himself if he thought this was strictly about Gavin.

He was simply not going to begin to accept failure. He planned to win. It was that simple. She was the nanny he wanted for his children.

The less simple part was how he was going to make her think she had won instead.

Not easy, but certainly not impossible. His new plan in place, he felt like whistling, though he refrained. Still, when he paid attention to that inner tune, he found the words lilting cheerfully through his head were, *How do you solve a problem like Maria?*

CHAPTER THREE

"I'D LIKE to submit my resignation," Prudence said bravely. She sat in the straight-backed chair in front of Mrs. Smith's desk. The weight of disappointing this woman who had believed in her was so heavy that she felt a little catch in her throat.

She'd been summoned here by a phone call at seven in the morning.

"Your resignation?" Mrs. Smith asked, obviously surprised.

Prue tried not to let her shock show. Her behavior of the night before had not been reported by the prince? Then why was she here? She had been holding the envelope that contained her letter of resignation firmly, now her grip on it relaxed slightly.

Still, there was no point in staying under false pretenses. Eventually Mrs. Smith was going to find out about the flower pitcher pitching incident. What if the prince was just a slothfully late riser, so filthy rich he didn't have to get up with the rest of the world? No doubt, that's what *real* princes were like. He probably just hadn't gotten around to reporting her yet!

Prue mentally added *slothful* to her Fatal Flaws List.

Then she took a deep breath. "I'm resigning because I

threw a vase at a potential client's head last night. It was most unprofessional, a total lapse of control, completely unacceptable behavior from someone representing the Academy." The devil inside of her insisted on adding, silently, *of Nine Fannies*.

Mrs. Smith's eyebrows rose. "Was anyone hurt?"

"No, I missed. I'm sorry." Naturally it came out sounding as if she was sorry she had missed.

Mrs. Smith seemed faintly distracted, as if she hadn't really heard any of Prue's confession. She knitted her hands together and looked at something beyond Prudence's left ear.

"I haven't always been Mrs. Abigail Smith," she said quietly.

"You haven't?" Prue asked, astonished. It had always seemed highly likely to her that Mrs. Smith had been The Nanny Maker for the last hundred years!

"Many years ago," she said quietly, "I lived in Russia. My name was Zivaa Plouffnikoff, and no one born and raised in the U.S.A. could even imagine such terrible times."

Prudence was not sure she would have been more surprised if Mrs. Smith had confessed to a sex change!

"I was given a chance to leave. It was one chance, and it was the chance every single person wanted. But I wasn't sure. I had friends. My mother was elderly. If I went would I ever see my beloved sisters again? Everything I knew was there. The chance was not without its risks and dangers. To me. And perhaps to them, too.

"But something in me whispered, *take this chance*. And I did. The road has not always been easy, and it has certainly not been without challenges. I buried a husband, but took the name he had given me, tamed my accent and reinvented myself. Out of necessity I created my Academy."

She sighed and was silent for a long time. "I have never regretted the decision I made that day so long ago. I wonder if I would have felt the same lack of regret had I chosen to stay in Russia."

Prudence realized Mrs. Smith wanted her to comment. "I think you always would have asked *what if?*"

Her employer looked pleased. "Yes, I think you're right. I think life invites us to journey outside of the land where we were born. To discover who we really are, we must leave the safety of the familiar. Have you ever done that, my dear?"

Prue felt that was exactly what she had done when she had decided to stop looking for the answers to her life in other people—specifically in male people.

"Don't you think I've done that for the past year?" Prudence asked. "I'm the perfect riches to rags story! I've been so far from the circumstances I was born to, I could have been issued a passport." And some days, it would have been officially stamped Hell. But other days, it had felt rich and good, as if she was discovering a secret long hidden.

"Hmm." Mrs. Smith sounded unconvinced.

"I love my work!" Prue stated firmly. The work had brought her out of herself. You could hardly remain the most superficial and self-centered of girls when your days were spent making mud pies!

"No, you don't. You love children. There's a difference. What you need, Prudence, is life that has some hope in it—some chance for self-improvement, betterment."

Prue frowned. She thought that was what she was moving toward. Should she tell Mrs. Smith about her work with Loaves and Fishes? And then she realized what Mrs. Smith was building to: a different version of Mrs. Hilroy's dismissal speech last night. It was time for Prudence to move toward a better future, blah, blah, blah. No, Mrs. Smith did not need her resignation when she was about to fire her. Prudence wondered if that would set some kind of record—being fired twice in less than twenty-four hours.

"I also think something in you is whispering right now, Prudence, telling you *take this chance*. Are you so stubborn you cannot hear it?"

"What chance?" she stammered, caught off balance since she had been bracing herself to be dismissed.

"Go to work for Prince Ryan Kaelan. Journey outside the land of the familiar—literally and figuratively. See what happens next."

"I don't think, after he had a pot of tulips hurtled at his head, he'll be begging me to go to work for him."

"It hardly seems sensible," Mrs. Smith agreed. She slid some papers across the desk.

"This is what he pays."

Prudence stared at the paper in front of her. Her mouth fell open. She felt sick to her stomach at the opportunity she had chased away. If not for herself, this kind of salary would allow her to make a real difference to Loaves and Fishes. She could personally "adopt" three or four people to provide meals to!

"That's a great deal of money for a nanny," she managed to choke.

"He says he pays his nanny the same as he pays his pilot, because both are charged with the lives of his children. He told me it was a point of principle. I wonder if you know how rare it is to find a man with those kind of principles?"

Prudence gulped. Oh, she knew all right. The offer was so

generous, his principles so honorable. She knew from her short experience minding other people's children just how very little value most people placed on the position.

Prince Ryan Kaelan valued his children! And the people who looked after them. Reluctantly Prudence remembered the look on his face when he had glanced at the picture of little Sara before handing it to her. Why couldn't she have thought of that before she let fly with the flowers?

Because she did not want to believe in princes! She did not want to believe anyone but herself could ever give her happily-ever-after.

"This is a picture of the suite that comes with the position."

Prudence stared at the photograph of a lovely apartment, sloped ceilings, large windows, a tiny, modern kitchen separated from a cozy living area by an eating counter with stainless steel stools at it. It looked like there was a private patio through open French doors off the kitchen.

She closed her eyes against her longing for a space exactly like that to call her own, and against the pain of what her stupid temper had cost her.

But what about her vow? What if he was all this, and had lips like those, too? A simple promise to oneself could melt under that kind of heat, so maybe he was the devil in disguise after all.

"He hires a secondary nanny so that his primary nanny can have evenings off, and weekends to herself."

On the other hand, what good was making a vow if it could not stand up to tests? Oh, not silly little tests like whether or not to smile at a desk clerk.

Big tests, like could she retain her budding sense of self around a man like Prince Kaelan?

The truth was she did not feel ready for the big test. She

would rather labor away for minimum wage. Clean houses. Wait tables.

No, she wouldn't.

"Ohmygod," Prudence moaned. "What a fool I am."

"Hold that thought when you meet him again."

"What?"

"Prince Kaelan is waiting in the conference room."

He was waiting in the conference room? Prudence's courage fled her. She would rather pass in her resignation. She laid it on the desk. "I can't see him again. Mrs. Smith, I yelled at him! I threw tulips at him! How can I possibly face him?"

I've made a vow to swear off my search for Mr. Right. One year with only myself. How can you keep a vow like that around a man like him? Even if he does have crooked teeth!

Mrs. Smith pushed the envelope back at her. "I would expect, even without being offered this job, you would want to face him, to have the opportunity to apologize to him. It would speak to your character." She sighed. "Though I'm afraid with that hair, you will always have certain challenges in the character department."

It didn't take long to find out just how challenged she was in the character department, because when Prudence opened the conference door and saw Prince Ryan Kaelan standing beside the long conference table, all easy confidence, exuding wealth and power and pure and unadulterated *arrogance,* she did not feel apologetic anymore. She found it very difficult to remember he was honorable and generous, and that he might be every bit the prince, inside and out, that he appeared to be.

No, instead it crowded her mind that he had interfered in her life! He had her dismissed from her job with the Hilroys!

He had been high-handed and self-centered, and acted as though she was a serf, bound to do his bidding no matter what her personal desire was.

That's what men did! Took over. Clouded reason. Moved you farther away from where you wanted to be instead of closer. He wouldn't be better than most! He would be worse! Because he was far too accustomed to power.

He looked up at her, and she was very aware of a battle between her logical self and that part of her that had gulped down romance like a drug ever since she was a little girl.

Her mind *wanted* to label him—high-handed or slothful or self-absorbed—it wanted to label him to protect her from the way her heart did a dizzying spin every time she was in the same room with him.

His eyes, so intensely blue, held some truth in them that made her stomach flip-flop, made her feel weak and power-less and vulnerable.

She shut her eyes and blurted out as quickly as she could, "I'm sorry for last night. I lost my head. Mrs. Smith claims it's an incurable trait in redheads and I agree completely. Incurable. I'm unsuited for any position in your household, so goodbye." As an afterthought, just so he understood she was being sincerely humble, she bit out, "Your Royal Highness."

And then she whirled and tried to escape out the door, thinking this was not quite what she'd expected. She'd tried very hard to think of the money, and the apartment, and yet, in the end it still came down to self-preservation. What was it about this man that made her so threatened?

She was not sure how he managed to get there first, but when she got to the door, he was already there, blocking her exit, his hand on the doorknob.

He was big and solid, and way too close to her. His breath stirred her hair, and she noticed the strength of his wrists.

If she loved him, she would buy him aftershave that smelled of smoky forests.

She shuddered, being pulled to a place she didn't want to be. He was interviewing a nanny, not a future queen!

"Why don't you have a seat, Miss Winslow? I just want a moment of your time."

He was blocking the door. When she wanted out. She bit her lip, and glared at his hand on the doorknob.

He moved it. To her chin.

Which was so much worse! Ever so gently, he tilted her chin up, forcing her to raise her eyes to his.

They held the splendor of tropical waters, and the heat of storms, and the complexities of sin.

If she loved him, she would write poems about his eyes.

"You got me fired from my job!" she said, so that he would never ever know how she saw poems when she looked at his eyes. She spat out the words in denial of what she felt with his fingers rested so lightly on her chin: her own vulnerability and his strength. What did she need to be strong for? His strength would be enough for both of them.

"I know I was responsible for having you relieved of a position you enjoyed. I will make everything right again."

It felt as though her breath stopped, as his words underscored that *feeling* that was enveloping her that she wouldn't have to do it on her own anymore, wouldn't have to try and hold it all together, wouldn't have to rely so totally on her own resourcefulness.

She tried to remind herself she liked self-reliance.

He spoke those words so softly and so solemnly he made

them into a vow. The intensity with which he was looking at her made her begin to tremble inside.

Oh, how she hated weakness in herself. If there was one lesson she had learned, hard and cruel, it was not to depend on anyone but herself to make her feel valued, worthy.

She had learned that when her father died, that she was alone, that the *thing* she had craved since she was a young teenager was not attainable in the real world, and that even if it was it could not fill the hole within her. It would be crazy to allow herself to believe her life, in one crazy flash of se-rendipity, could be made right again.

But if she didn't even listen to what Ryan had to say, wasn't she really saying the one she could no longer trust— had never been able to trust—was herself? To be strong? To be rational? To make the right choices? And do the right thing?

Who did she think she was, even thinking of him as Ryan? He was Prince Kaelan!

"Please," he said softly, and it was true he did not seem like a prince at all, but like a man a woman could actually dream of attaining.

I don't want to attain a man, Prue reminded herself. *She'd done that. She'd dated how many? A thousand? And lived with her fantasy until one exact moment. A moment she had planned and dreamed of and plotted for. The moment she kissed him.*

Each one of those thousand had fallen so, so short. It shouldn't have been so surprising. Many had flaws that had foreshadowed that they would fail her final test. Still, she would hope—and then her balloon would burst at the exact moment she had finally allowed lips to claim hers.

On the other hand, she couldn't live like a nun, cloistered safely away in a world where she did not have to face her own weaknesses!

The world was full of temptations. The idea was to be victorious over them—not to run from them. She was not doing this year-long journey to discover she was a coward! She must be sensible and listen to what he said. She had to trust herself to be *mature*.

He gestured to the table, and Prue went and sat at it. When he sat across from her, she folded her arms across her chest, and very *maturely* tried to pretend he had a fatal flaw: gross toenails, hair on his back, maybe those crooked teeth that managed to be so damned adorable came out at night.

"I come from a country where I was born into a position of command," he said slowly. "I realize it was presumptuous of me to come into your culture—with its history of rugged individualism—and try to make you do something you didn't want to do."

She twitched. He was supposed to be an *ass*.

"Exactly," she said crabbily. "Respect is earned in this country, not given."

"Though I think you may have made your decision not to work for me a little impulsively, and I'd like to think I can change your mind."

"Oh!" He was getting high-handed again, despite that oh-so-civil voice of his. *Arrogance the most fatal of flaws!*

"Are you going to stamp your foot again?" he asked, faintly teasing. "You're very, um, redheaded."

"I'm trying very hard not to be! I've been thinking of changing colors." Which she hadn't been until just this second. "Brunette perhaps."

"That would be a terrible mistake."

"It's a personal choice, and I don't need any help making it."

"I don't think," he said, a hint of a smile tickling at the sensuous full curve of his bottom lips, "you should ever try to be anything but exactly what you are."

She could not help it! She glared at him. The devil was in his eyes, after all, and his lips were twitching.

"That's the woman who threw a vase at you," she reminded him.

But his smile actually deepened.

"Do you find me funny?" she demanded.

"I'm afraid I do. Not in a bad way. Appealingly so."

This would be the wrong time to laugh—to give in to the spell, to be enchanted by this prince, by the humor that darkened his eyes to indigo ink, and by the smile that tugged at the firm line around his lips. Prue wanted to be respected, taken seriously. Laughing right now would be like thinking of Kelpie wrapped in toilet paper at her father's funeral.

So, naturally she laughed.

And he did, too. It was a moment of pure treachery—a moment when two people glimpse the startling fact they might have common ground, share a sense of humor, have those rare ingredients that can make people friends.

But for her to think that was indulging in her favorite vice, pure fantasy, so she folded her arms sternly over her chest and wiped the smile from her face.

"Will you allow me to show you a few things?" he asked quietly. "And when I'm done, if you still don't want to work for me, I will accept that. You will never see me again."

She was astonished by how the words struck her. Never see him again? It sounded like a finality she did not want to deal with. She became aware that a world where there was no chance of ever seeing him again—no chance of buying that aftershave or writing that poem—seemed like a very bleak place.

To be having these kind of thoughts at a job interview was worse than redheaded. She was having a full-blown love-junkie relapse! The only sensible thing would be to thank him again for his time, but to get up and leave.

Before *hope* took hold inside her, that Mrs. Smith had been right, and a whole new world awaited her, not her old world of pure fantasy, but a brand-new one, ground that she had never walked on before.

Naturally, since it would be the most sensible thing to leave, she settled herself just a little more firmly in her chair.

"All right," she said. "Show me."

And so he did. He laid a picture in front of her. Taken from the water, it was of an island, shrouded in mist, rising out of the sea. The impression was of luscious and abundant green, a sacred oasis of mystery and magnificence.

"This is the Isle of Momhilegra," he said. He said it *moh-veelagrah.* He began to flip through pictures, of roads that wound through green pastures, and stone houses, of cobbled village streets, and lonely mountain places, of waterfalls, of daffodils growing wild, of soaring cliffs, and giant majestic trees. The whole time he turned the pictures, he talked in a deep, reverent voice of his island home: its people, its climate, its industries, the most predominant of which involved music.

"Does it mean Isle of Music?" she asked, totally drawn in despite herself. His island was so beautiful it whispered to her very soul.

"Actually it doesn't. The name is Gaelic. It means *my thousand loves.*"

Now how unfair was that to the woman who had longed for just that thing? Who had looked for just that thing in a thousand faces she could no longer remember? The name shivered along her spine, like a touch. It made her think of romance, and places of the heart. It made her think of things she did not want to think of while sharing the same room as him.

"A surprisingly romantic name given the warlike tendencies of my ancestors," he said.

She could, unfortunately, see him as a warrior and that picture made her lick lips that had suddenly gone dry.

"So, is the culture Gaelic?" She thought she better make her mind move on from thoughts of him as the warrior prince who ruled that mysterious isle.

"The culture is a world unto itself. We are a little bit of Scotland, a little bit of Ireland, a little bit of Wales, some of England. We have traditions that can be traced to the Vikings, and we have some brand-new ones, like our annual Soap Box Derby, which has become a party for the whole island. Mostly, though, we are unique in all the world, a sanctuary very separate and distinct."

"And the government is a monarchy?"

"Yes, but it is a less structured form of a monarchy than, say, the British one. And it has always been based on the monarch accepting responsibility for the well-being of the people, not on the people accepting responsibility for the well-being of the monarch.

"Let me tell you how we got our first king. Hundreds of years ago, the island was ruled by a warlike clan, headed by a chieftain, Kaelan. Legend has it that Kaelan was summoned to see Arthur, the then King of England. Warlike or not, he knew he could not hold off a power like England if his tiny island had something that they wanted, and he knew it did, for the forests of the island were famed for the abundance and quality of their wood.

"And so before his visit, Kaelan promoted himself to King, in order to be on more equal footing with the man he would be meeting. And he brought with him what he knew they wanted.

"It was a lute made of the very special wood that grows only on Momhilegra. It is said that the instruments that come from our island all play enchanted music."

"And do they?" she breathed.

"It did that day. It is said Kaelan played the lute, and rather than becoming enemies, the two kings became friends and trading partners. The countries remain that to this day."

"It's just a legend, of course," she said, but her heart loved the story of something as whimsical as music mixed with magic bridging gaps and bringing peace.

"Of course," he said, but then he got up from where he sat, and reached under the table. He placed a plain case in front of her and opened it.

Inside was a lute, pear shaped, and very, very plain.

"It's for you," he said. "A time-honored peace offering, no matter what you decide."

"I suppose it plays enchanted music," she said, and heard the sharpness in her voice, knew she was struggling hard to contain some emotion so strong it threatened to strangle her. She knew, despite the simplicity of the instrument in front of her she was looking at something very rare and very valuable. She reached out and touched the wood. She had expected it would feel cold, but it did not. The wood felt warm beneath her fingertips.

He lifted the lute from its container, his motions slow and reverent. He put his leg up on one of the chairs, and rested the lute across his thigh. He strummed the strings.

The hair rose on her neck. She was not sure she had ever heard such a hauntingly beautiful sound before.

And then his fingers began to pick out a melody, simple, playful and sorrowful by turns, the music brought all the pains and all the pleasures of a thousand loves over a thousand years right into the room with them.

The music called her. It asked her to journey beyond any land she knew. It sang to her to embrace the unknown. It asked her to be brave. It told her to run toward adventure.

It whispered to her to trust.

Not him, not this man who could coax magic from a stringed instrument, but to trust herself.

"So," he asked, smiling faintly, setting the lute down, "does it play enchanted music?"

She knew exactly how Arthur must have felt all those years ago. He had known, just as she knew, you could not *take* that lute and have its music, for the music was joined intrinsically and inseparably to the spirit of the man who played it.

"It must," she said softly, reluctantly. "It must play enchanted music."

"So you will come to Momhilegra then?"

She could trust herself only to nod. She was going to the Isle of a Thousand Loves to be a nanny. That was all.

But with the notes of that music still hanging in the air, that was not how it felt.

It felt as if she had been adrift, and suddenly found shore. It felt as though a queen had been sleeping within her, and she had just awakened.

Dangerous thoughts, so far above her station and so out of line with her vow to be only pragmatic, she deserved to be slapped. Thoughts that were surely excuse enough to say no.

But she could not. She was caught in the spell of a thousand loves.

Prince Ryan Kaelan watched as Prudence Winslow signed the contract he had set before her. It asked her to commit to her new position for at least a year.

Today, her hair was up, and she was in a very businesslike suit—pin-striped blazer and trousers. She kept it from being entirely conservative by wearing a bright pink blouse underneath it that should have clashed with her hair, but it didn't.

Her tip of her tongue was caught between her teeth as she signed.

"I'm not sure why you are so intent on having me—"

The words hung for a long enough moment that he thought he was going to blush—dear God when was the last time he'd blushed—but then she rushed on, blushing herself, the red staining her fair complexion.

"—on having me come to work for you! I threw a container at your head in a fit of temper. Is that the role model you want around your children?"

"I'll try to refrain from making you that angry."

She shot him a look that was dubious, and he was aware her concern was a legitimate one. Prudence Winslow, despite that ever-so-mild-mannered name—was pure passion. Her true nature, impulsive, spontaneous, mischievous, rode ever so close to the surface, even now. He had seen each thing she was in her eyes as she looked at those photos.

Her eyes were the pool beneath Myria Falls: by turns

stormy and still, the calm surface easily rippled by the ever-present currents underneath.

In the end maybe that was why he wanted her. She was a woman who would throw vases, yes, but who would also throw herself in front of a car to save a child.

There was something elemental about her, as fierce, as strong, as real, as wind or rain or fire, and that is what he wanted for his children—someone who lived and felt deeply, who laughed and who cried. Who knew her own power well enough not to allow herself to be pushed around, browbeaten, by his five-year-old royal tyrant of a son.

He could not really hope to find those qualities on Momhilegra, where the family status created just a little too much awe, a little too much deference, even for the youngest members of the royal family.

Plus, all the nannies he had tried so far were too rigid in all the wrong areas. They had way too many ideas about what a prince's life should hold and not nearly enough about what a child's should hold.

Still, as he watched her sign those papers, Ryan was aware he felt inordinately pleased with himself, so maybe he was just kidding himself that this was about finding the perfect, passionate personality for his children.

Maybe it was really all about winning. She had said no to him. He could count on the fingers of one hand how many times he had been on the receiving end of that word in his life. He didn't like it. He hadn't accepted it.

Was that what it was all about, after all?

Ryan didn't like this one bit. He was a man who felt he knew himself, and suddenly to feel so muddy about his own motives, was unsettling. He hoped it wasn't a sign of things to come.

And yet as he moved toward her to take the papers she was holding out to him, he caught a sudden whiff of her scent.

He had smelled some of the most exquisite perfumes in the world.

She smelled of lemons and sunshine, and his senses felt absolutely capsized by it. It made him want to go and pull those ridiculous pins from her hair so it could scatter free around her face and shoulders.

Her scent, unfortunately, made his intentions feel muddier still.

This might have nothing at all to do with her being a fine nanny, or his inherent competitiveness.

No, maybe what he wanted so desperately for his children—laughter, spontaneity, someone who could be nothing but real—maybe those were things he had longed for himself as well.

He had a sense as he drew in the scent of her, as he looked into the Myria-green of her eyes, of something larger than him pushing him toward a destiny he could not predict.

He hated the feeling. He had experienced a destiny he had not predicted once before, when he had brought home a young bride, full of the expectation that she would grow to love him, and he her…

Still, he was reluctantly aware of liking the fact that maybe tomorrow held surprises he could not even guess at.

"So," she said passing him the papers, "what is the proper form of address for nanny to master of the castle?"

It was slightly irreverent, and he knew it was one of the qualities he liked about her. Sometimes, he just wanted to be a man, not the man who would be king.

"In private moments," he surprised himself by saying, "I

hope you'll feel free to call me Ryan. In not so private ones, the staff addresses me as sir. And what would you like me to call you?"

"Miss Winslow in private moments," she said, "and in not so private ones, ma'am." And she then laughed, and her laughter was robust, and full of the devil, and the kind of laughter who could set a man who had been in chains, free, even a man who had not even known he had been in chains.

"Kidding. Prue will do."

"Prue it is, then. An unusual name in this day and age."

She sighed. "I was named after a terribly wealthy aunt in hopes of currying her favor I'm afraid."

Though she said the words almost blithely, he did not care for the picture that painted of her family. To name a child for the gain it might result in? That was awful.

Though he was not sure, suddenly, if it was any more awful than powerful families arranging marriages with an eye to political and economic gain, rather than personal happiness.

"May I tell you some of my expectations?"

He was a little taken aback. He thought maybe the *employer* was the one who should be giving his expectations.

On the other hand, he might as well get used to things not going according to his expectations with her.

"By all means," he said, but he heard a bit of caution in his voice.

"It's just important to me that we both understand this— a nanny is temporary. A father is forever. My coming on staff does not mean that I don't have an expectation you will be a hands-on parent, prince or no prince."

A few minutes later, with his head spinning, Ryan realized

that he could add bossy and opinionated to his list of Prudence Winslow's character traits. She appeared not to be the least cowed by his station, and while he didn't want her to be, he was also not quite accustomed to being spoken to quite so directly.

After he'd said goodbye to her—she'd left clutching the lute case, even though he had told her he could look after it for her and deliver it to her new quarters—he found he had to sit down for a moment and gather his wits.

He smiled wryly to himself.

And he thought he'd won? The only one he'd been kidding was himself. She had a way of making him feel slightly off center, like a man who had survived an earthquake but had to look around to see if his world was the same as before.

And one thing he knew for sure, his world was not going to be the same as before once Miss Prudence Winslow was part of it.

And after fighting so hard to get her, why was he now so doubtful if this is what he wanted?

CHAPTER FOUR

PRUDENCE had grown up with wealth. She had attended private schools, lived in fine houses, had wonderful clothes, driven good cars, had fabulous holidays.

But as she boarded the private plane of the House of Kaelan, she was aware she had not grown up with this kind of wealth, and she was aware of the seductive pull and power of this lifestyle. It was nearly as bad as *someday my prince will come*.

It wasn't the *stuff*—she knew from experience you could feel as lonely in your Oscar de la Renta gown and Ferrari—as anyone else. She knew *stuff* had failed to fill the space in her heart, not that she hadn't tried.

Now, though in light of the fact she had experienced the real life adventure of trying to stretch a small pay check, this *stuff* represented a lifestyle of freedom—from worry, from the day to day grind, from struggles. Which brand of mac and cheese was on sale and seventy-five per cent off the winter jacket would never be a consideration in this world.

Prue sighed. She knew being poor had taught her more about herself than she had ever known when she was pampered. It had taught her she was strong and resourceful beyond her wildest dreams. Still, she felt the pull of all of this luxury and wealth, and her reaction startled her.

She was afraid. Would she lose that part of herself that she was just so recently finding?

The windows were all that gave away the fact it even was an airplane, windows, exit signs and the ever so subtle electronic Fasten Your Seatbelts signs. Now that she was looking Prue could see that there were indeed seat belts on those deep leather chairs grouped around a low round table in the first seating area.

The plane was divided into several areas—a theater area, an eating area, an entertaining area, a business area.

The color scheme was rich—subtle brocades in lush shades of caramel, brown and gold. Cushions provided splashes of burgundy. The carpets felt thick and rich underfoot.

Ronald came on behind her. "Let me show you where to stow your coat." Her liking for the dignified manservant only grew with every encounter she had with him.

He led her to a closet at the back of the plane, they had to pass two cabins, one on either side of the hall.

"They're bedrooms!" she breathed her shock.

When she peeked in the slightly ajar door, she expected to see an upgrade of a railway berth. Instead she saw a huge bed swathed in silk, sensuous as a sheik's hidden lair from the unrelenting sun. She looked away rapidly, hoping her cheeks were not on fire. She was fighting hard enough to hold her wildly imaginative romantic side in check without seeing the prince slept in a room that looked like that!

The other sleeping chamber was much plainer, two twin beds, quilts done in the same subdued, tasteful tones as the rest of the plane.

"Where should I sit?" she asked, trying to hide the shivering discomfort that brief look into the prince's airborne sleeping chamber had given her. "Is there a staff area?"

"I think, miss, you'll want to be with the family. That's where young Gavin will be, though I must say, I hope he sleeps. The long flight with the young lad can be a bit wearing." Still, there was tolerance in the way he shook his head.

She wanted to ask him everything there was to know about young Gavin. She had seen the boy so briefly, though it had been long enough to sympathize with that shake of Ronald's head.

She was on the verge of asking, but at that moment Prince Kaelan and his son stepped onto the plane.

It had been four days since she had seen the prince in Mrs. Smith's office. The whole time she had wondered if the sudden unexpected turn her life was taking could possibly be real. The rushed days of preparing to leave had a dreamlike quality.

And her thoughts of Prince Ryan had the same quality. At the oddest moments she would remember his voice, his scent, his eyes, and she would despise herself for remembering, and try to catalog his flaws instead.

It was a losing battle. She wondered if she was capable—after six love deprived months—of having made him up. Especially those eyes. Could any man—besides Matthew McConaughey—truly have eyes the way she was remembering them?

But now, seeing him again, she realized she had not imagined the eyes. If anything they were even better than she thought.

He was dressed in a perfectly fitted gray suit, with a slightly darker pinstripe going through it, the mandatory white shirt, a necktie that provided a surprising splash of color and hinted, just as the bedroom had, that there was a layer to the man that was private, passionate and not for public display. Still, he was a man who totally belonged to an airplane like this one. And his every movement radiated confidence, power, strength.

Seeing him again, she felt riddled by the self-doubts that had plagued her anytime she had stopped to breathe—which was mercifully not often—in the last four days. How could a woman—let alone one with her character defects—focus on her job around a man like that? How could a woman act normally? Remain professional?

Not daydream about eyes meeting, poetry and perfumes, long walks and linked hands?

Mrs. Smith had not covered problems like this one at her academy!

The plane seemed smaller with him in it, as if there was no place to escape the potency of him.

And how was it she was so easily able to forget his arrogance? Her ability to forget made her wonder how close she was to a complete relapse, a return to her former self, where she wasted her days dreaming of a man who loved her, a husband to hold her, of round-cheeked babies and a golden retriever. It was all a variation on someday my prince will come!

Gavin was at Ryan's his side, and she knew it was a sign that she was backsliding badly that she had not given the boy who would be her charge, her first and undivided attention.

Now she saw the poor child was dressed hideously—in a green velvet jacket with matching short pants, and a white shirt, white knee socks.

White! The whole outfit was ludicrous, made for portraits, not real life.

"Who chose the outfit?" she asked Ronald quietly as Ryan stowed a bag in an overhead bin that had been disguised as an ornate oak cabinet.

"I'm afraid I did. We've had no one in the nanny position. I struggle along."

Well, she could only hope from here on in, helping Gavin choose suitable clothes was part of her job.

"He'll be photographed getting on and off the plane," Ronald said, a trifle defensively.

"Of course he will," she said soothingly.

Still, small thing that it was, Gavin's needs had to come before photo opportunities. The outfit looked like a dusty royal relic, not even Haute Tot. It looked uncomfortable and impractical for a small child.

Then Prince Ryan saw her and smiled. His smile was everything she remembered—crooked—and still the smile of a man who could make a woman—even a cynical one slightly wounded by the circumstances of her life—long for fairy tales.

And it was the smile of a man who belonged in a bedroom like that one she had glimpsed, the unconsciously sensuous smile of a man who could take any woman of his choosing in there—

The prince had taken his son by the hand, and they stopped, now, in front of her. "Gavin, do you remember Miss Winslow?"

She knew her thoughts were not the thoughts of a proper nanny at all. The seduction she had felt when she entered the plane only got stronger around him.

Seduced by a prince.

Her heart felt as if it was going to beat out of her chest. Of course, that would never happen. He would not allow it. She would not allow it!

At least the Prue she had been for the past six months would not allow it. But *seduced?* Before her fantasies had ended with kisses, not seduction. Was it possible her affliction for imagining wildly romantic scenarios was progressing with deprivation rather than receding? She had to remind herself those scenarios *never* unfolded the ways she'd imagined them.

The truth was she wanted *perfection* so badly, she was still a virgin. She had never had one relationship progress past the disappointment of the kiss. Kisses that she'd anticipated, dreamed of, spent time orchestrating the arrival of: with roses and dinners and gifts. All leading to that one moment when she would *know.*

But so far, aggravating failure. After failure. After failure.

Kisses that were too wet, or too aggressive, or too passive, or too *nothing.* Kisses that could destroy a whole imagined wedding scene in one devastating slurp of a tongue where a tongue had no right to be!

Who was she now, today, after the last six months had stripped away every single thing she had used to define herself?

One thing remained that she knew for sure: she truly loved children, and they her. Not that you would know that from the way the wee Gavin glared at her! Children could be so fey— maybe he knew all about the renegade thoughts she was having about his father.

"She's going to be helping to care for you and Sara." Ryan said, and she appreciated how carefully he had worded this announcement.

Prue hated this moment. It was so awkward, though she

was glad she had not been introduced as the nanny. Gavin had that look of a boy who would detest a nanny.

Most children did. And it was not because they were naughty or difficult. Children, all children, wanted one thing so desperately their hearts nearly burst with that wanting. They wanted to be with their mom or their dad. There was a subtle message in handing over their care to a third party.

And it was *I don't have time for you.*

It was not the message any parent intended, and yet it seemed to be the message those fragile not quite formed hearts heard and felt.

Brian's first words to her, when she had initially been introduced to the Hilroy family had been, "I hate you."

And so, smiling, Prudence braced herself for that and held out her hand to Gavin.

"I don't think I recognize you, Gavin," she said gravely. "Though I saw a boy that looked a little like you once, but his eyes were crossed, which made him not nearly so handsome as you are."

Gavin was not charmed. He did not shake her extended hand, but thrust his own behind his back and glared at her more darkly yet.

"Go n-ithe an cat thu, is go n-ithe an diabhal an cat!"

Prudence tried to hide her shock. Did the boy speak gibberish then, his own private language? Why hadn't anybody told her that? She sent a frantic look at the prince.

But the prince's mouth had opened, and he wasn't looking at her. He stared at his son in astonishment.

"Where on earth did you learn to say that?" he demanded, not amused, or if he was, having the common sense not to show it.

She realized then what Gavin had spoken was not gibberish.

Gavin snapped his mouth shut, protecting the source, but Prue heard a faint cough behind her and glanced over her shoulder. Ronald, as well as the prince had understood perfectly what he said. Ronald was trying hard not to laugh.

"Never mind where you learned it," she said, "what does it mean?"

The child said nothing, looking back and forth between the adults with pure mutiny in the downturn of a stubborn little mouth that would someday be identical to his fathers.

She looked askance at Prince Ryan.

"I'm afraid its a curse," Ryan admitted, embarrassed. "An old Gaelic curse."

"Ah," she said. She imagined she must be very large for Gavin to look at, and even though he seemed unintimidated, she crouched down on her haunches, so she could be at his eye level.

"It's not a really good idea to say things unless we know what they mean," she said quietly. As she focused on the child, she was aware that now she was moving into a world where she was comfortable, and where she could feel completely herself, where she was untroubled by wild longings and imaginings.

"But I do know what it means!" Gavin spat out.

"You do?" She made herself look skeptical. "I don't believe it. How can a boy so young as you speak two languages? I don't speak two languages."

Just as she had hoped, Gavin puffed up at her flattery. "It means, *the cat eat you! And the devil eat the cat!*"

She had to fight very hard to keep her lips from twitching. She could not help but admire a boy with so much spunk.

Plus, his greeting was so much more original than Brian's more tried and true *I hate you.* She made the mistake of glancing at his father.

He was hiding his own twitching lips behind his hand. Ronald had disappeared and water was running somewhere, she suspected to hide his guffaws.

And she was very aware they were all was waiting— Ronald, Gavin and Ryan—to see how she handled this.

She stood up, but did not stop looking at Gavin. "I think," she said thoughtfully, "it would take a very large cat to eat me."

Gavin had not expected her response to be so mild, and he could not hide his disappointment that he had failed to goad her.

"It would," Gavin agreed reluctantly.

"I can't even imagine a cat that big!"

"Well, I can!"

"Can you? Hmm. No, I'm afraid I can't." She snapped her fingers. "Do you think you might be able to draw a picture of him? Otherwise I'm not sure I will believe there is a cat big enough to eat me."

Gavin considered this request with grave suspicion. "All right," he finally agreed, and Prue felt herself relax. She sensed the prince exhale beside her.

"Well, then, lets see about getting you settled, and then perhaps Ronald can show me where the crayons and papers are kept."

"I will need purple," Gavin warned her, just to let her know she wasn't going to be swallowed by just any old cat.

"Of course you will," Prue agreed, "and I would think some orange."

"Orange?"

"To show my hair in his mouth!"

"Oh, yes," Gavin said, gleefully, and then regarded her hair. "I will need lots and lots of orange."

"Let's go over here then, where there's a table, and as soon as the plane takes off, we won't waste any time."

"Will you be drawing a picture?" Gavin asked.

"Yes, yes, I will."

"Of a cat that eats people?" he said eagerly.

"No, that's too gruesome for me. I will probably be frightened enough just to look at yours."

"Yes, you probably will be," Gavin said with satisfaction. He darted by her. "Ronald do you know where my crayons are?"

"Indeed, I do, young man." They went off together.

"He's very articulate," she commented to the prince, watching the child, feeling a deep *liking* for him. "It's obvious he's had a great deal of time around adults."

"He was very rude!"

"It's not unexpected. Children don't want to be with a nanny. They want to be with their parents." Slipping into the comfortable role of nanny made Prue feel more secure, as if the flightiness was leaving her, and she was becoming grounded in what young Gavin needed, instead of worrying about her own needs, which were nebulous and hard to define at the best of times.

"In this case, you may be wrong," he said.

She heard some deep pain there, looked at him and didn't see a prince at all. She saw a man who had lost his wife and was struggling in a strange new world just as surely as she was. She felt something *real,* not fantasy, but a pure compassion for the man beside her.

"Your son loves you," she said. "Of this I am certain."

She had no idea where the words had come from, or why they had come out of her with such strength, but she was rewarded with a look of hope on the young father's face.

"Thank you," he said. "I hope you are right. And I'm impressed with how you handled your first skirmish with him. His last nanny used to threaten to clean his mouth with soap, but then she never followed through. Of course, she lasted less than a week. He crept into her room one morning while she slept and drew a moustache on her in permanent marker."

"Thanks for the warning. I'll keep the markers on the highest shelf, and I'll keep my bedroom door locked," Prue said.

"Good idea," he answered.

Two words, spoken with complete innocence, and yet she wondered just which prince she would be barring her door against.

"And the nanny before that left after a lengthy campaign of shenanigans the highlights of which include black shoe polish on the dog's feet, worms added to her luncheon salad and running away from her at a public parade downtown. Am I managing to frighten you?"

Oh, yes, he was. But not because of the antics of his precocious son! Because of the light in his eyes and the hint of laughter around the edges of his voice and the concern that ran like a subtle thread through his deep voice. Because she was seeing him as a man, with his challenges and problems, and not as a prince, and she was suddenly not sure which way of seeing him was more dangerous to her.

Thankfully it was the nanny in her that responded. "I get along rather famously with children and I have to admit I have a special soft-spot for the high-spirited ones," she said, *not to mention the ones who wore anger to mask some deep hurt.* "I'm afraid its adults I have difficulties with."

He regarded her thoughtfully, and then said softly. "I don't believe it. You could wrap anyone around your finger as easily as you did him!"

That mysterious *something* sizzled for a moment. Was that a challenge? "As long as I don't throw something first," she reminded him.

"Ah, well, yes, there's that."

A flight attendant came and asked them to take their seats as the crew was preparing for takeoff.

"I'm sorry," Ryan said, "I won't be able to join you. I have work to catch up on."

"Really?" Prue noticed Gavin had come back from retrieving the crayons with Ronald, but he stiffened at his father's announcement.

"What kind of work does a prince do, exactly?"

Ronald, crayons in hand, coughed, which she interpreted as meaning she wasn't supposed to ask, but then he wasn't supposed to be teaching Prince Gavin curses in Gaelic, either, so she didn't withdraw the question.

"My mother is officially the reigning monarch, but in the last few years her health has not been as good as it once was. Still, I tend to think of it as corporation. She's head of the board, my position is more like being the CEO. Though," he sighed, "Momhilegra would have to considered a very large and very unruly corporation."

"Well, perhaps when you're not too busy you could come comment on Gavin's cat," she said in an undertone as Gavin went with the flight attendant to be buckled into his seat.

She noticed how Ryan's eyes followed his son, troubled.

Soon after, she and Gavin were engrossed in their drawings, though she kept an eye on Ryan out of the corner of her eye. Almost as soon as the plane took off, he accepted coffee, loosened the tie at his throat, removed the suit jacket and rolled up his sleeves.

To reveal masculine forearms, muscled and tanned, that made her breath do funny things in her throat. Don't go there. *Moonlight. Wine. Soft music.*

Almost as if sensing her drifting attention, Gavin held up his drawing.

"There," Gavin said with satisfaction. "I'm done."

The seat belt signs had come off, so Prue undid hers and went and took the seat beside him rather than across from him. He accepted the closer position, thrusting the picture of a large and fierce-looking purple blob onto her lap.

She took a wild guess. "Are those teeth?" she gasped. Oh, this was the world she loved, a world so bright with potential and possibility, so vividly and wonderfully alive. Soon, she had forgotten all about the other prince.

"They are! Aren't they big?"

"They're absolutely frightening!"

Gavin chortled gleefully, grabbed his picture back, bent over it for a moment and added another row of fangs. "Ha ha," he said. "You're dead!"

"Well, perhaps not." She showed him her own drawing.

"That's nothing but a square," he said scornfully. "It's not even a good one. Your lines are crookedy."

"It's not a square. It's a box, and when I see that giant purple cat with his rows of gleaming fangs coming toward me, I'm going to climb inside this box and hide."

Prudence, she told herself firmly, *this is a worthy use of imagination.*

Gavin stared hard at her, and then at the box.

And then, so much sooner than she could have hoped, a boy just waiting for someone to come after him into the sad place where he had been trapped all by himself, he smiled tentatively at her.

And she smiled back and felt that smile, real and good, to the bottom of her toes.

Ryan tried to focus on his work, but he found it hard.

For four days, he had battled with himself. Had it been the right thing or the wrong thing to hire her?

He was aware that the *sensible* time to have that battle would have been before he had wooed her onto his team.

He was also aware, that for the first time in his life, he was in the grip of something that was, well, not *sensible.*

Prudence Winslow befuddled him.

And now he was her employer. Being someone's employer was a responsibility. It was a position of authority and of trust.

You couldn't be thinking thoughts about her hair and her eyes, and the way she had looked standing in a door, barefoot in a camisole with a jug of flowers in her hands.

The fact that he was a prince only heightened his every responsibility. He was watched by his family, his staff, the people of Momhilegra, the people of the world. His behavior had to be above reproach at all times.

He did not allow himself slips. No matter how tired he was, or how pressured he was, or how irritated he was, he did not ever act out in anger, frustration or impatience. He was aware he had a public image to uphold, and even those six years of marriage he had never failed—publically or privately—to treat his emotionally elusive wife with respect. No one had suspected their marriage was not blissful. The lack of response in her hand when he held it, the remoteness in her eyes when he'd smiled at her, that had been his private hell to endure.

But something about Prudence Winslow—the wild red of her hair, the flash of her eyes—threatened everything about him that was proper. Controlled. After six years of being tested, it felt like his immense capacity for discipline was near a breaking point.

This red haired vixen made him want to let go. Made him want to walk on the wild side, made him aware that he had a very secret side of himself waiting to be explored.

It was the side of himself that had seen her when he first got on the plane, and wanted to just gaze at her as if no other world existed.

It was the part of him that had wanted—when she talked of barring her bedroom door—to warn her that permanent felt markers were the least of her problems.

For he wanted to taste her lips, and touch her hair, and there was a part of him, long suppressed, that was as much a warrior as his long ago ancestors had been. And that part of him longed to clash with her, to fight with her, and then to subdue her and coax her willing surrender.

Go dtqchta an diabhal thu—may the devil choke you, he addressed this evil side of himself.

He sighed at his desk. He had always thought himself to be a strong man, immensely so. A man who knew what was required of him by the station of his birth, and by his loyalty and allegiance to his island nation.

He had done everything that had been asked of him, including his participation in a marriage that had been arranged for the greater good of companies and nations, a marriage that had nothing to do with people's hearts.

At the time of his marriage it had felt right.

At the age of twenty-two, already schooled in his duty, marriage based on the stirrings of a man's heart he would have branded as romantic hogwash. And still he had yearned, and hoped that with time and patience Raina would come around, if not to high romance, at least to a place where they could have been friends, companions.

If only she had told him her heart belonged to another before she had stood beside him at the altar. If only...

In such a short time, Prudence Winslow was stirring something in him, making himself ask questions he had never asked before.

Was he owed anything? Did he have any rights? Did he have the right to a life beyond the role he had been born to play? Was he entitled to know the fire of a man and a woman who felt passionately about each other?

But how could he, in his position, even explore those questions without someone getting hurt?

He glanced over at her. Her head was tucked in close to his son's. The hair was straining to be free from that ugly bun. She had dressed in a good outfit for traveling. It looked like wool, a dull shade of blue, a very sensible jacket and skirt, with flat black shoes.

Ryan hated it.

And he hated her hair like that, as if she had been watching *Supernanny* for her fashion tips.

He knew he had to get rid of her. If he was thinking

thoughts like this with her dressed like *that* he could not trust himself to do one sensible thing.

She had been right all along. He had been terribly high-handed with her life. What if he let her go now? After he had worked so hard to win her over?

He would compensate her richly, of course, for all the trouble he had caused her.

She would probably throw something at him.

And then it would be done.

But then Ryan heard his son laugh. Oh, it was a good sound. It was not the evil laugh that he had come to dread, either.

And he knew he was in a quandary, for she was the woman who could bring Gavin back to them.

If he had to steel himself against her while she did it, then that is what he had to do. Sometimes being strong, being a warrior, was not about taking what you wanted, not at all.

It was about acknowledging what you could never have, and being faithful to that which you had sworn allegiance to, despite the cost.

He remembered the promise he had made to go look at Gavin's drawing, and so steeling himself, he got up from his desk, and crossed the plane and sat down with them.

"Can I see?" he asked Gavin.

Gavin flipped his paper over on the table, hiding it from him.

It was his turn to be aware that Prudence was watching him to see how he would react. He was hurt, of course. Their laughter had beckoned to him, he had felt like a man who had been in the rain coming to a refuge with lights on inside and a fire burning. Now his own son refused him entrance.

Ryan, first in line to rule a nation, albeit a small one, found himself completely flummoxed by his son.

He met Prue's eyes, and found sympathy in them.

She pushed a piece of paper across the table, and the box of crayons.

"Perhaps," she said lightly, "you could draw something to show us."

He stared at the paper and the crayons, aghast. It had been years since he had been involved in such silliness. Since he had been a boy not much older than Gavin was. Draw a picture? Of what?

He was going to refuse, and go back to work, but he saw that Gavin was looking at him, for the first time in many, many months with reluctant interest.

He picked up the crayons, and chose a purple one. He drew a purple mouse, not that it looked much like a mouse.

He gave it to Gavin. "There. It is something for your cat to eat when he gets hungry. Much better than him eating Miss Winslow."

Gavin studied the offering very seriously.

"Well," he said finally, tucking the picture behind his own, "he might get hungry, as Miss Winslow—"

"Prue, please!"

"Has drawn herself a box to hide in."

"She has? May I see it?"

Prue looked as shy as if he had asked to see her underwear, but she passed him her drawing.

It was terrible. A square.

And yet Ryan saw immediately what she had done. She had gone to Gavin's world instead of asking the boy to come to hers.

He felt astonishing relief. Because over the past few days he had asked himself if he had lost his mind in hiring the temperamental Miss Winslow. He had tormented himself with the question. Even moments ago he had entertained the notion of firing her. For his own comfort, for his own peace of mind.

It bothered him that he was questioning himself. He made decisions, sometimes dozens of them per day, quickly and efficiently. He did not second guess them, and he did not look back. He rarely had the luxury of that kind of time, even if he had been the kind of man who looked back, which he was not.

But now, looking at this plain drawing, he knew his heart had been telling him what to do when he had hired the nanny who had thrown a pot of flowers at his head. His doubt was so intense because he was not a man accustomed to hearing the language of the heart, let alone listening to it.

He was a man who listened to his head. But suddenly he saw that language, rational, sober, pragmatic, had failed him where it counted most. It had failed him in reaching a wife who did not want to be reached, and now when he needed to help heal his small, tremendously hurting young boy. Had Gavin learned from his mother to retreat rather than confront?

He looked at Prudence Winslow again.

The faintest smile was playing across her lips. He noticed her lips were puffy and full, incredibly, sinfully sensuous. Lips that begged a man to kiss them.

His stomach felt like it was on a roller coaster ride, and not because the plane picked that moment to hit an air pocket, either.

It was because his heart had things to tell him yet.

But could a man of his age learn a brand-new language?

It would take a kind of bravery that he had not asked of himself before.

CHAPTER FIVE

"GOOD night, Prue-loo." Gavin wrapped his sturdy arms around her neck, pressed his cheek into hers. He smelled of his bath, and freshly laundered jammies, the sweet smells of innocence.

Prue wondered what other job on the face of the earth gave benefits like this? And how could she, after only one month, love this child so much? It wasn't that there hadn't been challenges, but if anything his sensitivity and rebelliousness only made her love him more. Like, tonight, for instance, he was trying to hide the fact his father had hurt his feelings, but she could see it in the faint bruised look in his dark eyes.

"Good night, Gavin McWavin."

She stopped at the door and blew him a kiss. He blew her one back, but she detected it was halfhearted at best. She went and checked on the baby, fast asleep in her crib, thumb in her mouth and fanny in the air. She smiled at Idelle, the night nanny, a sweet girl of nineteen, who had already settled at a desk in the playroom with her studies, and then went across the hall to her own quarters.

Her rooms were beautiful, bright and cozy. Now, she went to her small, tidy kitchen, made a cup of tea and then went and stood at her window. From there she could see green pastures, fringed with trees, sweeping down to the sea. The moon was out tonight, and waves capped in silver exploded into fairy frost as they hit the ragged rocks of the shoreline.

She had arrived in Momhilegra in the dead of night. Even in the blackness, the island had whispered to Prue. She had been able to hear the wind in the ancient trees, and smell the crisp fragrance of the island forests, mingled with the scent of the sea. The mild air had wrapped around her, like a blanket or an embrace. Her first glimpse of the castle, lit up, turrets soaring darker than the night, had literally taken her breath away.

Nothing had disappointed. Her quarters were lovely beyond what the pictures had shown her. Her relationship with Gavin grew stronger every day. It was true, he could be headstrong and difficult and stubborn, but he was just a little boy, who had built a fortress around a hurting heart. Her first instinct, that he had been *waiting* for someone to break down those walls was proving to be true.

And from the moment Prue had taken the cooing sweet-smelling Sara into her arms it had been love, of the truest sort, pure and intense.

In many ways life was satisfying. She had free rein of the children's quarters, and was busy rejuvenating them from stuffy quarters more suited to an aging bachelor uncle—a wealthy aging bachelor uncle—to a living space suitable to two lively children.

Unwilling to ask for anything else, wanting to give things to the children that were from her, not part of her job description, Prue had started using some of her own extremely generous wages to buy the children play clothes. Gavin now had jeans and T-shirts, Sara had hardy red overalls that she shouted for each morning.

The island during the day was unbelievable. She'd had several days off and Prue explored her new land by bicycle. She loved the free concerts at the multitude of music schools, she had lined up with the tourists to see the lutes being handmade at the instrument factory, she loved the charming little shops on the main street of Morun, pronounced moh roo-in, capital of the island. Just a ten-minute bike ride from the castle, Prue could buy handmade chocolates and home-knitted sweaters, exquisitely well-made and hardy clothes for the children.

But what she loved most about this island was how it was steeped in tradition. People who lived here had a deep sense of belonging, they were connected to their pasts. They knew who they were. They loved fun. Right now the whole island was preparing for the huge influx of visitors that would arrive for the annual Soap Box Derby. Every father seemed to be out in the yard with his son, hammering away on go-cart creations. Sometimes she would even catch glimpses of fathers with their daughters building.

That called to a girl who had experienced every material possession, but who had longed for a sense of belonging, a sense of family, more than anything else.

On another day off, far from the busy hammering of fathers and children, she had ridden her bike in the other direction away from Morun, through rolling green hills, lush pastures, quaint farms. In half an hour she had found herself in the deep coolness of the woods. In those solitary hours spent in the woods, Prue had been astonished to find she felt deeply alive, and wonderfully connected.

She had been happy all by herself! She had felt the wonderful tingle along her skin that she had thought she would feel only if she was in love with another person!

It was mystifying, freeing, wonderful…and troubling.

Gazing out her window now at the mysteries of a dark ocean exploding into foam on the rocks, Prue knew she had everything she had ever dreamed of.

And yet a strange restlessness ate at her. For if one thing did disappoint, it was Prince Ryan Kaelan.

At first he had made an effort to be the hands-on father she had asked him to be. He was an awkward father, better with the baby than with Gavin. Still, he had gamely tried. He read bedtime stories, joined them for lunch, tried to play board games.

But lately he had withdrawn, claiming there was an enormous amount to do for the upcoming derby. Prue missed him more than she had any right to!

And here was the plain truth of the matter—in New York City, and even as she had jetted here—despite the obvious opulence of his lifestyle, the crests, the servants—she had really had no idea what it meant, precisely, that Ryan Kaelan was a prince, the next in line for the throne of Momhilegra.

Here on Momhilegra, it was impossible to forget.

His mother was officially the reigning monarch. Prue brought the children to visit her several times a week and was taken with her gentleness and quiet wisdom. But it was sadly obvious that she was failing. It was the prince who was the most integral part of island life. Schools and streets were named after him. The most popular name for baby boys on the island was Ryan. He had understated things—severely—when he had said his position was like being a CEO of a major company.

He was the CEO and the patron saint. He was the spirit and

the lifeblood. The prince was busy every waking moment: attending to business or attending concerts, officially greeting visiting dignitaries. He was the honorary head of every organization from the Momhilegra Women of Music to the Momhilegra Soccer Team. The upcoming Soap Box Derby bore his name and he seemed to be involved in the smallest details of making it happen. The people of the island, the staff of his household, the local government officials—everyone— loved him. No it was more than love, the prince was devoted to, revered.

The local news station had at least one story about him every night, and the weekly paper was always peppered with his photos. And he was a photogenic man! Prue could not get away from his image—head thrown back in laughter as he was presented with a toy dragon; kneeling beside an old woman in a wheelchair, both her hands caught in his; throwing nets with the local fisherman, easy grace in every line of his powerful build.

From Idelle, Prue had learned tourism was the island's number one industry, and from the young woman's tales of the prince's popularity, it seemed to Prue many of those tourists were exactly like those women waiting at the elevator at the Waldorf. They were waiting for a glimpse of the prince. And, according to Idelle, he more than gave them what they wanted. He showed up, unannounced at outdoor cafés to shake hands and talk to people, he rotated through the evening music concerts giving opening remarks, he was known to show up at the lute factory and play one of the brand-new lutes— which then was sold to a thoroughly enchanted tourist for an astronomical amount of money. Idelle said the staff were busy getting the royal go-cart ready for Derby day.

It was very hard to kill the *someday my prince will come*

fantasy while actually sharing a life with a real live one! And just like those eager tourists—or those women who had waited at the foot of the elevator—she found herself, disgustingly, waiting to catch a glimpse of him, to have a few moments with him.

And, in terribly unguarded, undisciplined moments, dreaming. *A horse drawn carriage. Him bowing before her at the ball.*

But lately, in his heavily scheduled life, he did not seem to be scheduling in specific times for his children. Rather, he squeezed them into available moments. So, he might show up unexpectedly for breakfast, or for playtime, or to say good-night.

Prue was all too aware of feeling that the sun came into the room with him. Ryan Kaelan was pure charismatic energy. It was in the flash of his slightly crooked smile, the easy power of his movements, in the way he cocked his head ever so slightly to listen to her answer a question he had asked, or to listen to a joke Gavin had to tell, or to listen to Sara babble incoherently and gleefully into his ear.

And he was unconsciously, damnably sexy.

Everything he did, whether it was tossing his daughter in the air until she shrieked with delight, or picking a piece of bacon off a platter on the table and eating it with his fingers, had a bigger than life quality about it, made Prue's chest ache with *something*.

Weakness!

Because, despite his charmed existence, all was not well in the kingdom Momhilegra. Prue could easily see that Ryan's relationship with Gavin was strained. Did he actually avoid his son because of that strain? And there was something in his eyes, in unguarded moments, that she saw that she thought maybe no one else did.

He was lonely beyond what most people could endure.

Or was that just part of her own fantasy? That the lonely prince's eyes would one day light on her, and his heart would come awake?

Utter foolishness, because seeing him here, on his turf, in Momhilegra made her realize what an important man he was, made her acutely and painfully aware of the difference in their stations.

On the plane, she had managed to forget that. Gavin had gone to bed and the prince had invited her to join him in the theater. They had watched a movie together, a light and thoroughly implausible romantic comedy.

A simple thing, really, a man and a woman watching a movie together.

It had been easy to forget they were on his private jet flying to *his* island. As they had laughed over the movie and shared a bowl of popcorn it had become even easier to forget that he was a monarch.

And that she was a servant.

She had liked the ease between them, she had enjoyed that suspended moment in time when they shook off their roles, and were just people. She had not been troubled then by fantasies of happily-ever-after. No, she had been, for once, just totally immersed in the moment. And it had been fun.

But here on Momhilegra it was more than obvious to her the opportunities for the nanny and the prince to have fun together were going to be few and far between. It was in her face every single day that Prince Ryan Kaelan was far from an ordinary man.

And it was in her face very time she saw him—playing a quick game with Gavin, tossing his daughter in the air, his laughter ringing through the nursery—that a longing, was growing within her, dangerous and untamable as the hunger of a lion who had not been fed.

It was in her face that the old longing was back, worse than ever. This time she was longing for love from a man who was beyond her reach.

She realized now she had sensed this danger from the very first, and had done everything in her power to fight against it—even thrown a vase of flowers at him.

Leave me alone. She had literally hurled the message at him.

But he had not. He had not heeded her.

And now the feelings she was having for him—secret and intense—were affecting the way she did her job.

Because she had warned him she expected him to be a hands-on parent, and if this was his idea of hands-on it was not acceptable to her. In the last two weeks he had averaged less than twenty minutes a day with his children.

She had clearly outlined her expectations that day in the conference room at Mrs. Smith's and now she had not followed through.

She had not followed through out of self-protection. She had not followed through because she was intimidated by his status, and his importance. She had not followed through because she was sadly aware of her own weaknesses.

She had not followed through because if she insisted he spent more time with his children, then he would be spending more time with her.

That one evening flying here, laughing, chatting, wonderfully comfortable with each other, had ended. One evening, and when the prince had said goodbye she had felt like a fish removed from water—removed from everything it needed to live—when she had realized they would not be sharing moments like that often, maybe even never again.

How could she ask him to have more to do with his children when his presence made her ache for things she could not have?

And how could she not?

How could she ignore, any longer, the fury in Gavin's eyes when on a night like tonight, his father called to say good-night when Ryan had promised he would come in person?

An important meeting he said on the phone, sincere regret in his voice.

But then Gavin would not even come to the phone to say good-night to him.

Gavin's relationship with his father was puzzling. He seemed to yearn for Ryan's attention, and yet when he received it he rebuffed it.

Her job, Prue reminded herself, was to insure the well-being of her young charges.

Not her own well-being.

It was easier for her if the prince was not overly involved with his children. It was easier for her because she did not have to catch the intoxicating scent of him, did not have to see the brightness of his smile, the quick play of muscles as he lifted up his daughter.

It was easier because then she could love them with her whole heart and soul without asking herself what the price was going to be of loving these children so much.

But she could not tolerate it anymore. The way these children felt about themselves, and about their place in the world was at stake. As lovely as it was to redecorate their rooms, and buy them clothes, and accept their growing affections, that was not what they needed. Sara and Gavin needed more of their father. If it proved too difficult for Prue to handle more of him—if she began to feel like she would choke on her yearning for happily-ever-after *with him*—she would have to leave.

But her gift of love—her legacy to Gavin and Sara—would be to do her best to insure the children had a working and loving relationship with their father first.

Setting down her tea, she went back across the hall and smiled at Idelle, who was scowling at her studies. Prue tiptoed back into Gavin's room

He was asleep, his beautiful lashes dark spikes against his round cheeks.

But he was clutching a stuffed cat she had bought him in one of the Morun shops. She had been unable to resist when she saw it was purple. Sadly, as she drew near to him, she saw Gavin's cheeks were stained with tears.

More disappointed that his daddy had not come to say good-night than he wanted to be?

Or a little boy who still missed his mommy very much?

His mother's picture was on the stand beside his bed, a raven-haired beauty in an ivory formal gown. In the photo Gavin on her lap, in the hideous green suit. The picture, unfortunately was posed, and Prue had a hard time reading the woman's face, though her eyes seemed to be looking off into the distance. Could Princess Raina possibly have held that little boy on her lap and been as sad as she looked?

Prue bent and kissed the sleeping child's face once more, then straightened knowing she could not put off her duty to these children for one more moment.

Tonight was the night. The prince's cavalier attitude toward his children had to be addressed. This was the latest incident, but not an isolated one.

She glanced down at herself. She was in jeans and a sweater. Her hair was down, and her makeup had worn off hours ago.

Part of her wanted to go and change into the new silk slack suit she had gotten in Morun. Part of her wanted to try to tame her hair. Part of her wanted to refresh her makeup so that her eyes looked as green as the water at the bottom of water falls she had stumbled across one day while exploring.

But she knew that made it about *her*.

And she also knew if she waited, if she took those precious moments to primp, the surge of adrenaline she was feeling at this moment might abandon her. If she waited for the perfect moment she might lose her nerve.

She also knew she had to build up a head of steam, she had to try to erase those images of the prince that made her feel weak, like a woman so in the grip of wanting fairy tales to be real that she would just allow any kind of behavior.

Here was the truth: Ryan the High and Mighty had broken a vow to his son. How dare he tell Gavin—promise him—that he would come say good-night and then not come?

It's not as if the prince was in another country! He was right over there. When she looked out her own bedroom window she could see the wing of the sprawling stone castle that he was in. It would have taken him half an hour to come and say good-night to his precious, fragile children!

He was too important for that? What could possibly be more important to a man than his own children?

He was filled with self-importance! That was his problem! All this adulation from the populace of his island kingdom had swollen his head.

She added *self-importance* to her Fatal Flaws List.

Prince Ryan Kaelan was about to encounter a problem like none he'd ever had before. She could not become one of his adoring legions, no matter how tempting it was!

This whole move to this island was about temptation! About facing her own dragons, and putting them to rest! There was no better night than tonight!

Prue stuffed her feet into the nearest shoes, closed her apartment door and headed down to beard the lion in his den.

Prince Ryan's head ached. He glanced at his watch. He had been in negotiations for twelve hours. His suit jacket and his necktie were strung across the chair back behind him, his sleeves were rolled up. He wished these negotiations had not been scheduled for this week, when the Derby was less than a month away and that needed his attention, too.

Still, he sensed, with a predatorlike instinct, that the other man was weary, too, and that he was very close to getting what he wanted.

It was a lucrative contract to join the name of Momhilegra with a marketing firm that wanted to use the royal crest—the dragon wrapped around the lute—as a seal of approval on certain musical events, recordings and instruments. Of course, the negotiations were extremely delicate. The prince had to have guarantees and measures of control that would protect the reputation and integrity of Momhilegra. The marketing firm did not want to give him everything he needed.

The prince was aware the money he was being offered was secondary to the publicity the liaison could generate if handled properly, but he shrewdly wanted as much of both as he could get. And he wanted control.

Still, Mr. Marchand was proving a difficult man. Not impossible, but difficult. Ryan could sense something changing in his attitude now. The next few moments would be crucial.

There was a knock on the door, and Ryan felt annoyed. He had sensed how sensitive the next hour was going to be, and he had instructed Ronald they were not to be interrupted.

Ronald came back from the door now, leaned over him.

"Miss Winslow," he whispered.

Prudence? But did that mean something had happened to one of the children? Negotiations forgotten, he rocketed from his chair, leaving Ronald to explain his sudden departure to Mr. Marchand.

Prudence was out in the hallway, pacing, her back to him.

"The children? Are they all right?" he asked. He touched her shoulder, and she spun around.

As always, he felt that certain breathlessness, that he did his best to mask. He jammed his hands in his pockets, rather than give in to that overwhelming desire to touch her hair.

Which was down tonight, scattered wildly around her face. He had been avoiding her for this very reason. His children needed her, were flourishing under her attention like flowers that had needed rain. He was so aware how easily he could spoil it for them, take from them what they needed most, by complicating his relationship with her.

He saw the answer to his question in her eyes. There would never be any such thing as a simple relationship with her, and the children were fine.

The anger flashing in her eyes, turning them to green flame, was directed at him. He slid a look around for stray vases or other things not nailed down. He wondered what on earth he had done to deserve her wrath.

"How would you define all right, Your Royal Ryan the Important?"

He had a million-dollar deal falling apart in the room behind him! Now was not the time to feel amused at her impudence. Delighted by it. In fact, he felt almost as if he had waited for this, when she had been so prim and proper in each of their meetings, such a perfect and utterly *boring* nanny.

He folded his arms over his chest, a battle stance. "How would I define if my children are all right? Are they breathing? Not bleeding?"

"Well, if that's how you'd define all right, I suppose they're fine by your book! I suppose if a little boy crying himself to sleep is all right with you, then they're fine!"

His heart fell, and he dropped his arms from his chest. "Gavin cried himself to sleep? But why?"

"A certain high and mighty man promised he would say good-night to him, and then phoned in his apologies instead."

"I wanted to explain to him. He wouldn't come to the phone. And you didn't make him!"

She raised her eyebrows at him and said softly, dangerously, "You thought I should have made him?"

"Yes. That's your job." Though he wasn't sure that's what he thought at all. He just had an unholy liking for this sport of crossing swords with her.

"If you're unhappy with my performance please say so now."

But of course he was not unhappy with her performance. He had seen new light in Gavin's eyes, the bounce returning to his son's step. The nursery quarters themselves seemed to be filling with sunshine, and it had nothing to do with the yellow walls and the friendly dragon cavorting across the wall mural. It had nothing to do with a bed shaped like a car replacing the four-poster antique model that had been the childhood bed of the future king of Momhilegra for centuries.

He could not threaten something that was so good for his children for the simple pleasure of bickering with her.

He let his defenses drop, reluctantly. "I didn't think it was that big a deal to him," he admitted, "whether I came or not to say good-night. Gavin doesn't act like he much cares when I do come. On occasion, I have felt he hates my arrival."

"He is a boy who has lost his mother," she said. "He needs to know there are things in this world he can trust, and you need to be that thing. When you say you are going to do something with him, that needs to be sacred to you."

Perhaps it was because it was true, Ryan felt so stung. He found his arms folded across his chest again.

"So, you've come and taken me from a very sensitive negotiation to tell me this? To dress me down like a junior officer under your command? You couldn't have the common courtesy to wait until morning?"

She did not flinch from his reminder that he outranked her! And then some.

"That's right," she said without apology. "And no, I did not feel it could wait. Those children are my job, and they are quickly becoming the most important thing in my world. I cannot understand how they could not be the most important in yours!"

Her condemnation of him cut to the soul. And yet, he had known this was exactly what he would get from the moment he had first seen her picture, her body crumpled in front of that car.

He had hoped he would get a woman who would defend her children with her very life. He had just not expected he would bear the brunt of her devotion!

He was genuinely flummoxed. Annoyed. Intrigued.

No one on Momhilegra had ever dared speak to him like this. He didn't like it. And yet part of him sighed with relief, a strange sense of homecoming.

Finally, finally, someone who would be true.

"Your son needs you," she said firmly, and her tone softened.

"He doesn't act like it."

"It's up to you to overcome that," she said. "He's five years old. He doesn't know how."

Prince Ryan Kaelan was sadly aware that he was a man who knew how to negotiate million-dollar contracts, lead people, make laws. He was a man who knew the future of his small island nation rested solidly on his shoulders, on the decisions he made, and he accepted that responsibility. His life was complex, full, meaningful.

And yet if the mysteries of a small boy's heart evaded him, then was he a failure? He had never felt a sense of failure before, and yet that is what he felt when he looked into the blazing accusation in Prudence's eyes.

As if he had failed at what was most important of all.

How could he know the hearts of others when his own heart was such a mystery to him?

On the flight here, with Miss Winslow, it had called to him.

Every time he saw her it called to him.

And the truth was he was doing his best to ignore it.

"I don't know how, either," he said, his voice stiff with pride and hurt and stubbornness.

She drew close to him. He saw the fire in her eyes, and wondered if she would slap him. He was aware he would almost welcome the sting of her palm against his cheek, because her passion called to a place deep within him, that he liked even as he denied its existence.

But she did not slap him.

Though what she did had the power of a slap.

She touched his bare arm, above the wrist, her fingertips gentle, her eyes suddenly soft with compassion.

"Will you let me show you?" she asked.

He realized she was not just talking about showing him how to make the voyage to his young son's heart. She would sail him across uncharted waters to a world he had never entered.

A world where he would not always be in control.

A world where a man could get hurt.

Or be reborn into a different man than he had been before.

Once you had crossed those waters, could he ever return to the safety of this land? He glanced back at the closed door of the conference room.

That was his old life and it beckoned him, like the glow of the lighthouse bringing the sailors in from sea.

But some sailors turned away from that safe glow, and set a new course, to worlds they had never been to before.

The bravest did that. The bravest of the brave.

"All right," he said slowly. "Show me."

"Spend the day with us tomorrow," she said. "We'll take the children on a picnic. I found a place in the woods where there is a waterfall."

He knew that place. He had gone there often when he was a boy. He had been enchanted by the magic of it, he had loved the freedom of going there by himself, in a world where he was too seldom alone, when even then, in the days of his boyhood, so much had been required of him.

He knew how to smile when his heart was elsewhere. He would wear the best of suits, when he longed for dungarees. He would attend the opening of the school of stringed instruments, even when the string he most wanted was the one that drifts across clear green waters, a hook attached to one end of it.

Oh, he knew that place, where he had gone when things were too hard.

When he was told, as just a lad, not to dream dreams for himself. He would never be a pilot or a fisherman or a fireman.

When he was told he would not be allowed to travel, unescorted, with friends to camp for one week in the Australian Outback.

When he had been told who his wife would be, a woman he had known since childhood, whom he liked and respected and had thought he would come to love.

How could Prudence Winslow have found Myria Falls so soon after coming here?

And could he go there with her?

To the place where he had laid his personal dreams? And his personal hopes? And his personal ambitions? It seemed every one of them probably lived there still, in that glen of mist and rainbows.

He had not been to Myria Falls for a long, long time.

It would be madness to go to such a place with a woman who reminded him of things he could not have.

"I'm sorry," he said, suddenly, curtly. "My business here will not be concluded by tomorrow."

Her hand fell from his arm. She nodded, and curtsied, that curtsy somehow more loaded with scorn than if she had thrown another vase at him, or slapped him.

And then she turned and ran, and though she did not turn and look back at him, he sensed she was crying.

Because he had disappointed her.

All the people he had never disappointed, who owned pieces of him, and he had disappointed her.

Sighing, he went back into the meeting. He was distressed to see he no longer cared about the details of the contract. His focus was diluted. His clarity was gone. The contract seemed ridiculous in light of the fact a small boy had cried himself to sleep tonight.

Another small boy, many years ago, had taken his tears to a grotto, his tears of disappointment. Had he not vowed then his own children would not have the same life he had?

And yet here they were. Here they were, and he was not doing the right things by them.

Simply put, he did not know how. He had never learned it.

But his nanny had offered to teach him. To show him. He understood, suddenly, he was standing on a precipice.

He had told her he would not go, but he was aware he had not made his final choice yet, and that the choice he made, though it seemed small to the point of insignificance, really had the potential of changing his life forever.

CHAPTER SIX

"PRUE, you are not paying attention!" Gavin said, standing at his chair at the kitchen counter in her apartment.

She turned and looked at him and smiled despite the fact she felt tired and distracted.

It was true, she mustn't have been paying attention. Gavin had peanut butter smeared from his ear to his cheek.

"You're right, love," she admitted. "I wasn't."

And the reason she wasn't was that her stomach felt hollow with disappointment over Prince Ryan's rejection of her invitation last night. She had hardly slept, reliving the humiliation of that moment when she had been so sure he would say yes to her, and instead he had said no.

In a way, she tried to tell herself now, it was a good thing. It would be far too easy to get caught up in the prince-mania that had this island—and perhaps the world—in its grip. It would be far too easy to give into that thing inside her that so *wanted* to be the heroine to his hero.

Not that she had any right to be thinking of him as a hero. This was the reality: she barely knew him. She had made the mistake of falling under the spell of his charisma, but the truth was he possessed quite a number of items on the Fatal Flaws List.

"Prue! For the one hundredth time does the peanut stuff go on the cracker first, or the jam?"

"Yes," a deep voice said from her doorway. "Age-old questions. Which comes first? Chicken or egg? Peanut butter or jam?"

She looked up. Prince Ryan was leaning against the jamb of the open door of her suite. His lips were quirked upward slightly, but his eyes held an intensity that was indeed ageless, and which asked her all kinds of uncomfortable questions about men and woman. Which came first? Love or chemistry? Could one be mistaken for another?

"Peanut butter," she said quickly. "Put the peanut butter on first."

The prince was dressed more casually than she had ever seen him, in black slacks and short-sleeved shirt that might have looked like a golf shirt, except it was the royal emblem on the breast. She had suspected an amazing build, now she could see the hard bulge of muscle in his forearms and biceps, and in the place where those casual slacks clung to the large muscle of his thigh.

And she was dressed in an extremely childproof velour track suit, in a shade of pink that did nothing for the hair that had been pulled back into a careless ponytail.

The way he was dressed made him look like an ordinary man, a man that a woman in pink velour might aspire to.

Then he smiled, and ran a careless hand through the dark silk of his hair, and she knew there would never be anything ordinary about him, overlapping teeth notwithstanding.

"Prince Ryan," she said crisply, and formally, "how may I help you?"

"I came to accept your invitation. I would like to join you on your picnic after all."

But she was suddenly very aware of the danger of him. She had felt something thrum to life within her the moment he stepped in that room.

Asking him to spend more time with her—with his children—had been like playing with matches, playing with sparks of light and heat that she had no hope of controlling if she allowed them, even once, to touch something combustible, to flare out of control.

With him leaning in her doorway, watching her with those sooty, sensual eyes, she knew darned well what the combustible ingredient was, too! It was her!

Flustered, she dropped the knife on the floor.

Good sense screamed at her: *cancel the picnic.* But as she straightened, she saw that Gavin was stealing a glimpse at his father. There was something guarded in his face, and yet right behind that barricade was a wistfulness, a hopefulness.

Which is why, she reminded herself, she had talked to the prince last night in the first place.

For the sake of his children.

"Delighted to have you," she managed to mumble, though what she was really feeling was so much more complex than that! A day with him? A whole day of sunshine, and children's laughter, and sneaking peeks, and being so tautly aware of him?

What on earth had she been thinking when she had gone to see him last night? Mrs. Smith would be quick to point out to her that was the problem with redheads! They simply could not be counted on to think things all the way through!

"You'll have to help, then," Gavin told him, his tone distinctly unwelcoming, though that was not what Prue had seen in his eyes.

"I will?" Ryan said good-naturedly, and came into her small quarters.

Her tiny home lost its feeling of sanctuary in an instant. Now that he had stood at that counter, would it always feel like something was missing when he was not there? Would she stand at this counter, alone, and feel a strange discontent, a restlessness?

"You will have to help make lunch," Gavin said imperiously.

His father was looking at the crackers on the counter, the lumps of brown goo that Gavin was spreading a little too vigorously on them.

"Couldn't we just order something from the kitchen?" he asked dubiously. "What is this?"

"It's peanut butter," Gavin told him officiously, though ten minutes ago he had surprised Prue by not knowing what peanut butter was himself.

"Is it edible?" Ryan asked. "It looks like, er—"

"Poo!" Gavin crowed.

Ryan's mouth twitched. It was evident he wanted very badly to be stern. But then he gave in, and laughed. Gavin laughed, too, even though it was evident he wanted very badly not to. It was such a delightful moment, the two princes, who had probably never dined on anything less than roast snipe, eyeing the peanut butter with suspicion.

"Have you tried it yet?" Ryan asked his young son.

"I'm a bit scared to," Gavin admitted.

"Me, too." And then they were chortling together again.

Such a simple moment—exactly the kind of moments the father and son needed many of together.

"If you try it, I will," Ryan told Gavin.

Gavin shook his head. "No, you first. I insist."

And then they were both laughing again.

Sara, in her playpen just off the corner of the counter did not like being left out of the merriment. She hauled herself up on the side of the pen, and jumped up and down on pudgy legs.

Her father went and lifted her with easy strength, planted a kiss on the curve of her neck.

"Have I seen this outfit before?" he asked, and Prue knew red overalls on the princess were right up there with peanut butter on the list of royal have-nots.

"Give some peanut butter to her," Gavin suggested.

"No!" Prue said. "No peanut butter for the baby. She's much too young. I've packed a bottle for her and some baby food. And," she added sternly, "there's to be no sampling of the crackers until we get to the picnic place. When you're good and hungry you'll both eat them."

"Yes, ma'am," Prince Ryan said with mock deference, and Gavin grinned.

Together they stood at the counter packing the lunches. It was a simple moment, a domestic one, surreal given the company she was in: two royal princes and one royal princess. Despite the fact she knew this was not reality for this family, that this was an illusion engineered by her, Prue was not unaware of the sharp yearning inside of her to have moments like this.

Would she ever? Or was this what she had sacrificed when she had agreed to come to Momhilegra, her opportunity to have a normal life?

You have never had a normal life, she reminded herself sternly.

She glanced at Prince Ryan, and amended the thought. Maybe what she had given up was her opportunity to ever be *satisfied* with a normal life.

That point was driven home a little further, when Prince Ryan took them out to the back courtyard. Waiting for them was a little cart with a sturdy brown and white pony hooked to it!

Ordinary people did not go on picnics in pony carts! But at that very moment, Prue made a decision to forget ordinary and just enjoy every moment of the extraordinary experience that she was being given!

The horse drawn carriage of her dreams was about to become a reality.

Once he had them all settled in the cart, Ryan leaped up beside them and took the reins.

Prue quickly found out riding in a pony trap was hardly going to be about the romance of a bygone day. Ryan was directing the pony across country, and Prue had to hold on for dear life just to make sure the baby did not bounce out of her lap! Her bottom teeth felt as if they were going to be driven through the roof of her mouth. Her kidneys began to hurt.

And then she laughed out loud: this was exactly what she needed to remember. Fantasy and reality were two very different things!

Ryan grinned at her. "Having fun?"

And strangely enough, she was! The pony took them through places where a car could not go. The clip-clop of his hooves was lovely and mesmerizing. Plus, Ryan now had Gavin standing between his legs, and the young boy had taken the reins. His face glowed with happiness as his father's arms went around him, showing him how to command the pony.

Wasn't this one of the things Prue was coming to love

about Momhilegra? It was a place, in a world that had lost its traditions, this was a place steeped in them.

A place where the ancient secrets and music and traditions were passed from one generation to the next.

A place where pony carts had been driven for thousands of years, and where men passed on this skill to their sons.

They drew to the edge of the forest, and Ryan unharnessed the pony from the cart.

"Won't he run home?" Prue asked, relieved to once more be on solid ground.

Ryan laughed. "Look at what a stout little fellow he is, and look at this pasture full of spring grass. No, he'll be here when we get back, and he'll have barely lifted his head from the spot where he is right now."

Their worlds were just so different. He knew about the behavior of ponies, he knew the secrets of ancient music. She knew about peanut butter. But she had promised herself she would just enjoy this day, as it was offered, that she would not spoil it by over analyzing.

Prince Ryan took the baby from her, Gavin ran ahead of them down a narrow but worn dirt trail that wound through the deep darkness of the forest.

The little boy would get ahead, hide behind a tree and then jump out at them, shrieking with delight at how he managed to startle them each time.

"You've been good for him," Ryan told her.

"Not as good as he has been for me," she admitted.

In a short time the woods opened to a clearing, a grotto of lush grass and ferns and wildflowers. There was a green pool, surrounded by large smooth stones, and at the far end of it a waterfall cascaded down its mist weaving with the rays of sun to make rainbows.

Even the baby stopped babbling, and became silent. They shared the awed silence of those in the presence of one of the wonders of the world.

"Sometimes," Prue said out loud, "reality is better than anything you could ever imagine."

They set down the picnic things, and then they played: hide and seek among the giant trees, and tag, until they were all breathless with laughter.

"I'm hungry!" Gavin finally announced.

Prince senior and prince junior attacked their crackers with enthusiasm. She had never seen anyone sampling peanut butter for the first time and she would not have missed the experience.

Lunch was almost done when Gavin sniffed the air.

"Sara stinks," he announced with disgust.

Prince Ryan looked terribly uncomfortable, as if someone had had the bad manners to bring an elephant to a royal luncheon.

"I'll just leave you to it then," he said scrambling to his feet, as if that elephant had begun to rampage.

So, finally the time had come to turn the prince into a mortal man. Prue took a deep breath, though she then regretted it. Sara smelled horrendous!

"Just a cotton-pickin' second," she said before Ryan could make good his escape. "Have you never changed a baby's knappy?"

"I happen to be a prince," he told her sternly. "That excludes me from knappy changing duty."

"Well, not today it doesn't." She got to her feet, too, and

faced him with her hands on her hips. She could almost hear Mrs. Smith—*oh, Prudence, he's a prince*—but she managed to ignore her. She needed to know who he really was, and somehow that meant getting him out of his comfort zone.

"Imagine fathering two children and not knowing how to change a diaper!"

"You are not going to ask me to change that diaper!" Ryan said, astounded.

"Yes, I am!"

"Don't do it," Gavin warned his father in an undertone, "it's gross."

It was the first time she had seen a teaming up of the father and son, and they both glanced at her now with identical formidable expressions, the stamp of the father so unmistakable in the sudden warrior like cast of Gavin's face.

Powerful in battle she reminded herself.

"I think I'm going to pass on knappy changing lessons," Ryan said.

Gavin nodded his approval.

Prue was in an awkward position now. It was, despite the casual couching of the words, a royal refusal.

"In fact," Ryan said, "I'd rather do about anything else."

"Slay dragons," Gavin suggested.

"Exactly."

She could see how much alike they were, almost of one mind. Why was it they were not getting along? What was the rift between them?

Well, that was for later! Right now, the little princess was growing stinkier by the second!

"I understand perfectly," she said with a smile. "You're scared."

Ryan frowned at her.

Gavin glared. "My dah is not scared of anything!" he proclaimed. "Are you, Dah?"

Prue shot Ryan a look. He was obviously very pleased about the endearment. Gavin usually addressed him quite formally as Father. Never Dad, or Daddy. Still Prince Dah looked very displeased about the position he had backed himself into.

"Everyone's afraid of something," he told his son.

"But not a diaper!" she pressed.

He glared at her, Gavin looked at him expectantly.

"Oh, give me that baby," Ryan said.

"Here you go, Princess Stinky Pants. Your royal father wants to see you."

Ryan took her gingerly. He held her at arms' length.

"I'm not watching this," Gavin said. "I might chuck my peanut butter." He wandered over to the pond and began trying to skip stones off its calm surface.

"Me, too," Ryan muttered, then glared at Prue. "It's not kind to unman a person in front of his son." He put the baby back down on the blanket, on her back, knelt over her.

"Oh. Did it say somewhere on my résumé that I was kind?"

"As a matter of fact, it did not!"

"Good. So the first thing you do is undo that snap on her leotard."

Begrudgingly, with a gingerness at odds with the masculine strength he exuded, Ryan did as he was instructed. Sara cooed at him and wagged her chubby legs in the air.

He made a face at the odor being fanned at him and snatched her legs, quickly dispensed with the rest of the leotard.

"Now what?" he asked tersely.

Prue tried very hard not to laugh. Powerful in battle indeed! "Now you undo that little tab right there. And the one on the other side."

"Good Lord."

"You can't hold your breath that long," she warned him, noticing his voice was getting strained, and his face was turning red.

"I intend to try."

The redness drained from his face suddenly. He was ashen as he confronted the contents of the diaper. Was he going to faint? Prue would probably be declared public enemy number one if she made Momhilegra's most beloved son faint! She giggled.

Ryan glared at her. "Gavin, come hold my nose," he shouted.

"No!" Gavin shouted back.

"Oh, never mind," Prue said, trying to stifle giggles and taking pity on him. "At least you tried. I'll finish up."

But now she did see the warrior in him. He glared at her with such furious resolve that she almost stepped back from him. The laughter died in her.

"I don't quit," he said.

Oh, yes, she should remember that. "Okay, then, I'll hold your nose."

She was sure there was probably a law somewhere on Momhilegra that you were not allowed to hold the prince's royal nose, but if there was he wasn't going to mention it.

She studied the situation, trying to figure out the best angle.

"Hurry up!" he snapped at her.

"Yes, Your Royal Highness."

"Oh, sure, you wait until now to recognize my station!"

She went behind him, crouched awkwardly over his back, felt for and found his nose.

She squeezed.

"That's better," he said. His voice came out in an unfortunate nasal tone.

The giggle came back.

"Don't make me laugh," he warned. "I'm pretty sure laughing involves inhaling."

She was aware of how she was draped over him, of the fine feel of his strong back beneath her breast. She was aware that all she could smell was him, and that he smelled of heaven— tangy, like the forest, mysterious like the sea, and sensual like the pure man that he was. His scent overrode the unpleasant odor wafting off the baby.

"It's off," he choked out, "now what?"

"I said I can finish."

"And I said I am not being defeated by this!"

"Okay. Reach for those that plastic container over there. It has wipes in it."

"Don't you let go of my nose."

"Well, that's going to be very difficult."

"I don't care."

And so she did her best to stick with him as he leaned way over to get the wipes. She pressed into him even more intimately, her breasts flattened against his broad back as she balanced precariously on one leg trying to shadow his movements.

He paused and she knew the exact moment he realized there was a little more happening here than he thought. She waited for him to tell her to undrape herself from his royal hide, but he did not. It felt as if he was holding his breath yet again, and then he began to breathe.

His hand found the wipes, and she moved back with him.

An entire container of wipes later, and three tries with the new diaper and he staggered to his feet, and held the baby triumphantly, the lion king presenting his prodigy to the jungle.

Unfortunately Princess Sara wiggled, gave the tiniest little grunt, and brown liquid squirted out the saggy side of the ineptly placed diaper, and right onto Prince Ryan's royal shirt!

His look of triumph evaporated and was replaced with one of abject dismay.

He thrust the baby at Prue, and then tearing off his shirt as if acid was burning through it, he raced for the water.

"It's going to be cold," Prue tried to warn him.

He didn't seem to care if there was ice blocks floating in it. He pulled off his slacks one leg at a time, still running.

The laughter died in Prue's throat. Ryan was now wearing tartan boxers and nothing else. His body was lean and strong, and very nearly naked. She was not sure if she had ever seen a more beautifully made man.

The truth was, for all the richness of her fantasy life, she had never been this close to a man with nearly nothing on! Her wildest imaginings had not prepared her for this. Unlike the pony cart, which had not lived up to the dreamed-of version, this was more powerful than she would have believed possible. It felt as though it was her turn to stop breathing. Some dragon that had slept within her blinked awake, stretched, breathed a little fire…

Thankfully the prince dove cleanly into the water. And his head emerged moments later, across the small pond, nearly under the waterfall. He stopped and shook diamond droplets from the darkness of his hair, and he let out a shout.

It was a cry as primal as the place they were in: exuberant, deeply male. It could be the cry of fearlessness that a warrior issued before battle, an embrace of life.

The sound that came from him—wild, masculine, powerful—moved up and down her spine like a physical touch. The dragon roared, his breath making an inferno in the bottom of her belly.

She turned away quickly to tend to the baby. But she was aware her movements were an automation—she was really focused intensely on Prince Ryan.

The water felt wonderful, icy cold and bracing, exactly what a man who had been losing his head needed: a slap.

For rising to the challenge of changing the diaper certainly ranked as one of the most atrocious events of Ryan's life.

So, why had it been once Prue's hand had touched his nose, that he had barely noticed the horror of it? Once he had become aware of the way she was touching him, draped over him, her every exquisite curve pressed into him that soggy diaper had very nearly disappeared from his consciousness.

Firsts today. He had never eaten peanut butter. He had never changed a foul diaper.

And he had never felt so on fire as he had in that moment of accidental intimacy: weak with a kind of longing, and at the same time tremendously feverishly strong.

It was a good thing the baby had leaked on him. It had given him an excuse to do what he needed to do: cool off, gain control.

And yet the cry that had just come from his mouth was not exactly the cry of a man in control.

And suddenly he did not want to be that man anyway.

He saw what Prue was offering him, what she had offered him from the beginning.

Respite from the godlike status imposed on him by his title, by his islanders, by the media, by a world gone insane for any whisper of celebrity. It was so damned wearing.

Prue Winslow offered him the chance to be what he longed for most in those moments of loneliness that he had been born to bear, but that weighed on him, sometimes, as though he carried stones on his shoulders.

Prince Ryan Kaelan longed to be an ordinary man.

"Come in," he called to Prue from the water. She was fussing over the baby, rechanging the diaper. He knew, of course, she couldn't come in. What would she do with the baby? But he liked teasing her.

She could hide nothing from him it seemed, for he saw temptation flash through her eyes, before she gave him a withering look.

"That would be most improper!" she said imperiously, playing along as if she had a choice to swim with him and was refusing it.

"Improper?" he crowed with laughter. "I think improper was when you threw the vase at my head."

She looked regal, as if she had forgotten that event entirely.

"I think improper was when you called me Royal Ryan the Important last night."

She turned quickly from him, and picked up the baby, apparently to remind him of what her duty was.

"I think improper was making me change a crappy diaper."

"I don't think princes are allowed to say crap," she said.

It was true. Princes were not allowed to say crap.

Nor should they be quite so *aware* of the hired help. Prue

settled herself back on the blanket, looking regally indifferent to him, but he knew, with a kind of joyous male knowledge that she was not the least bit indifferent to him.

Ryan did the most ordinary of things, something every teenage boy and young man in the world—except him—had done. He showed off for the beautiful woman watching him. He did a strong stroke under the waterfall, he lifted himself up on the rocks, and climbed high, high above the falls.

"Get down from there!"

Her shout could barely be heard over the roar of the falls. But he heard it, heard the real concern laced with the reluctant admiration she was feeling for his bravery.

"Yes, madam," he called, and then he threw himself way out, as he had done dozens of times since finding this place when he was a boy, and he somersaulted over the edge of the waterfall, and hit the freezing water cleanly.

He surfaced to bask in her admiration at his prowess.

Instead she was not even looking at him.

"Gavin, stop!"

Her voice held panic in it, and Ryan saw his young son stripping off his clothes on a rock near the edge of the pool.

He raced over, and caught Gavin as he leaped into the water.

"It's cold," Gavin shrieked joyfully.

"Yes, it's not for the weak-spirited," Ryan agreed.

His son was clinging to him, and he could not believe how good it felt after the months of remoteness that he could not understand, the censure in the boy's eyes.

They played in the water until he noticed Gavin's lips turning blue, his teeth chattering.

Prue was already on the edge, holding the baby in one arm, and the picnic blanket in the other.

He handed Gavin to her, and she wrapped the blanket protectively around him and gave Ryan the stern look one might expect from one of Mrs. Smith's nannies. "He'll probably catch a cold," she said. "It's much too early for swimming."

"You don't catch colds from being cold," Ryan told her. "You catch them from viruses. The men of the House of Kaelan have swum in these waters since the ice was off of them from the beginning of time."

"Humph." She looked like she was trying to be unimpressed, but not really succeeding. But he noticed his son enjoyed being grouped with the men of his family.

Ryan climbed out of the pool, and stood before her, the water sluicing off his naked, chilled skin.

Her eyes were the hungry eyes of a lioness.

But her mouth formed a little "O" of astonishment, and she turned away.

He pulled his trousers back on, but he was not even going to save that shirt.

He grinned at her, when she turned back toward him, her cheeks stained with fire and with knowing. Something as ancient as this grotto was between them.

They were a man and a woman. And something called to them that was older than time.

And he was glad.

For his entire life he thought this was what he had sacrificed: the fire that most men got to feel. Now he saw it was not so, and he felt reverence for her, as if she was a goddess who had been brought to him to restore the life force within him.

But then the wider picture came into focus, his son wrapped in a blanket, teeth chattering, clinging to her thigh.

His baby girl in her arms, her thumb in her mouth, her eyes fastened sleepily on Prue's face, so trusting of her.

He realized the situation he found himself in was devilishly complicated. For he wanted nothing more than to lean over and capture the full redness of her bottom lip between his teeth. But If he took what he wanted from her, what price would it cost them, his children?

He was pulled back into his old life, his own life, with a snap.

Every decision he'd ever made in his whole life had to be carefully measured, the repercussions thought through and evaluated.

He could not be a man who could just lean forward and kiss the woman he found beautiful.

So, perhaps it was in rebellion to that, that he did it anyway.

He took advantage of the fact Prue's hold on the baby left her in no position to back away over the mist-slicked rocks around her, and in no position to push him away, either. He leaned forward toward her, his intent clear.

"No!" she whispered. "You have terrible toes. Terrible!"

He looked down at his toes, puzzled, and looked back at her. "You don't want to kiss me because of my toes?" he said, astounded.

"That's right," she said.

"Kiss?" Gavin wailed. "You canna kiss Prue!"

Ryan was not sure that her flimsy toe excuse could have stopped him. He was not even sure that she really wanted it to. But Gavin's cry of dismay stopped him cold.

Ryan broke reluctantly from the complexities of Prue, and turned and looked at his son.

Gavin was watching them intensely, his face a startling

shade of white, and not from cold, either. He was staring at the man who had fathered him with such abject fear that it nearly tore Ryan's heart from his chest.

CHAPTER SEVEN

PRUE stared at Prince Ryan Kaelan. She had almost been kissed by a prince! In an enchanted grotto. Not even she had ever conjured up a kiss this wildly romantic! It was a moment she had waited for all her life, the kind of moment a girl—even one who had made a vow—could get lost in. The heat in his eyes, the way his lips had parted slightly, the clean scent of him as he had leaned toward her…

Had her prince finally come? Or, if their lips had met, was she the one girl on the face of the earth completely capable of turning a prince into a toad?

Was that why she had held up Fatal Flaw #14, bad toes, like a shield in front of her? It was true she had always hated bad toes—where the second one was longer than the first one—but it had seemed insanely flimsy at that moment when he had been leaning toward her!

Maybe the truth was that she was glad that kiss hadn't happened. She didn't want to know if Ryan would fail the kiss test as surely as every man before him. She realized, shocked, she didn't want to dream of a future with him. She didn't want to plan imaginary meals, long walks, elaborate weddings.

And the reason she didn't want to do it was that it might

wreck what she had just enjoyed—simple moments of hide-and-seek, tag among the trees, and peanut butter on crackers.

The reason she didn't want to place Ryan at the center of her happily-ever-after fantasy was not just that she had sworn off happily-ever-after fantasies.

It was that she had an opportunity to help him, and a kiss between them might steal that opportunity away, might alienate Gavin even further from his father.

She followed Ryan's gaze and sure enough Gavin stood watching them, white-faced, nearly trembling with anxiety. The wall he had constructed against his father had come down, just a bit, just for a few moments, but now it looked like Gavin fully intended to rebuild it.

Prince Ryan's son was afraid of him.

Ryan looked baffled and hurt by the expression on his son's face. In this frozen moment, he was not so much a prince as an ordinary man lost in a new world, the foreign land of single parenting. Not his status, or wealth or his kingdom could help him negotiate this place where he found himself, floundering.

Prue realized, her heart breaking for him, that Ryan knew as little about finding his way back to Gavin as he knew about changing that diaper.

Looking at him, at the sorrow and confusion that altered his handsome features, Prudence shivered. It was a moment of revelation, and it was like the sun coming out on a soul that had been shrouded.

She realized this was not about her. It was not about whether she could find her prince. It was certainly not about whether he could pass the kiss test!

That was not why she had been brought to this enchanted

island at all. It was about whether or not she could find herself, her true character, her ability to rise above her most human yearnings, and walk with angels.

She realized, with a sense of great relief, that she was all done looking for a hero, that she had finally arrived at the place where she wanted to be when she had, by some instinct—unsure of where it was leading, but knowing she had to go there all the same—made that vow to herself to take a year off from the desperate manhunt.

She was not looking for a hero. Her quest was done. It was finished with this startling truth: Prudence Winslow was going to be the hero.

She was going to lead Ryan back to his son.

She was going to show him how to build the bridge between their hearts. But how? It was not as if she was any kind of expert on families, and certainly not on intimacy.

But she was an expert on lonely children, and she knew what each lonely child wanted most of all.

To feel valued. To feel assured of their place in the world. To feel safe and connected. And then inspiration came as surely as that feeling of revelation moments ago. And she knew exactly how to do it.

"Well," she said cheerfully, "let's pack up the picnic things and get back. We have urgent things to do."

Both princes scowled at her with identical skeptical expressions.

"We do?" Gavin and Ryan said together.

"We do," she said firmly.

Gavin was suddenly mutinous. "I am not done throwing rocks," he announced, and looked between the two adults who had wounded him. It was probably very natural that the young boy would feel a betrayal of his mother in the fact that his father had been about to kiss another woman.

"As a matter of fact," Ryan said, imperiously, "you are done throwing rocks!"

"I'm not!"

Prue could see this situation was going to deteriorate quite badly if given the chance, so she could not give it the chance.

"Gavin, your father is going to help you build a go-cart for the Soap Box Derby."

"He is?" Gavin said, rocks forgotten, his eyes wide.

"I am?" Ryan said.

"We're going to have to hurry. The Derby is coming up quickly. Is it only three weeks away? I believe there is a special category for boys under six."

"I'm going to be *in* the Derby?" Gavin breathed.

"If your *dah*—" she used the term of endearment casually and deliberately "—can figure out how to build you a cart."

"Oh, he can," Gavin said, and the fright of earlier battled with pride in his eyes. His interior skirmish was blessedly short. His hand crept into his father's. "You can, can't you, Dah?"

Ryan shot her a look over Gavin's head, loaded with self-doubt. But he said to his son, with calm certainty, "Of course I can."

Gavin wasn't completely won over, though, because he let go of his father's hand instantly and then he chose to ride in the back of the cart, rather than on the seat beside his father.

As they were driving the pony back to the castle, Ryan leaned over to her and said in an undertone, "I hope to hell you know how to build a go-cart."

"Are you allowed to say hell?" she teased him. "I'm afraid I haven't reached that chapter of my royal protocol book."

"Under certain circumstances I most certainly am! Do you know you have an aggravating way of changing the subject instead of answering the question?"

"I do know, Your Royal Highness," she said demurely. "And, no, I'm afraid I don't know the first thing about building go-carts."

"That figures," Ryan said, but with good humor. "And I want to know what's wrong with my toes."

"They're flawed," she said. "I'm sorry. You'll have to accept that. We all have flaws."

"Are you kidding me?"

"No, I'm not. Has no one ever told you you had a flaw before?"

He was silent, and then he said thoughtfully, "Actually I don't think anyone has." And then Prince Ryan Kaelan threw back his head and laughed and it was really just about enough to make a woman totally forget he possessed such royally ugly toes!

When they arrived at the castle, Ryan lifted Gavin down from the cart, tucked Sara under his arm as an afterthought.

"Could you look after the pony?"

"But I don't know anything about ponies," she said, but she was saying it to a departing back. Ryan grinned fiendishly at her over his shoulder. Ah, payback from the man who knew nothing about go-carts! And probably for the insult about the toes, too!

The pony, who she had thought was cute to the point of being angelic, took a nip at her as soon as they were alone, then broke out of her grasp on his headstall, hurried over to the flower beds and began gobbling down the royal blooms!

When she tried to catch him, he neatly swung his head at her, and toppled her onto a rosebush. Then he trotted the cart right up into the bed, leaving a wide swath of wreckage in his wake. She scrambled to her feet. She tried to lure him into thinking she'd given up by concentrating on picking thorns from the seat of her pants. When he seemed to be totally engrossed in lopping the head off a particularly rare looking orchid she lunged at him. He shied sideways and took out an entire bed of begonias.

Prue was finally rescued by a groundskeeper who had looked like he wanted to weep at the damage that had been wrought.

Still, he had managed to laugh when Prue shouted at the departing pony, being led away by a stable boy, *"Go n-ithe an cat thu, is go n-ithe an diabhal an cat!"*

Then she noticed she was being watched. There were two faces at the open nursery window on the second floor. How long had they watched without coming to help her? Ryan gave her a smirk and a half wave when he saw he had been noticed.

"And same to you!" she shouted at him shaking her fist.

The two heads disappeared, but the groundskeeper was staring at her with his mouth open, as if she was the devil who had swallowed the cat who had eaten the disobedient pony!

"Miss," he said uncomfortably, "you canna curse the prince."

"I didn't directly. Besides, he's just a man," she informed him, and her anger seemed to have evaporated. She actually felt cheerful.

Her rescuer looked appalled. "He is our sovereign," he corrected her stiffly.

"Well, if you think he's so perfect you should have a look at his toes!" How lonely a life Prince Ryan led. Being surrounded by adulation must be a terrible thing!

She entered the nursery to find both princes drawing furiously, the baby sitting on the table between them, nibbling happily on a crayon.

Prue rescued the crayon from her. "Crayons make for very colorful poop," she told Ryan sternly, her hands on her hips. Sovereign or not the man was in desperate need of some daddy lessons.

"How's your, um—"

"Bum," Gavin filled in gleefully. "We saw you fall in the roses. Does it hurt?"

"No!" she said. "Okay. Maybe just a bit."

"I can help you. With the thorns," the elder prince offered.

"You can help me with the thorns, but you couldn't help me with the pony? You knew he was an evil-spirited beast when you turned him over to me!"

"Didn't."

"Did."

"Careful. Don't curse the prince!" he warned her, apparently having heard that part of the conversation, too.

"Oh! You are impossible. And you have ugly feet!" The prince looked delighted by the pronouncement rather than insulted. She removed her attention from him, since he seemed to be delighting in it so much. "Gavin, show me what you've done so far."

"We are making a blueprint! 'Cept they're not really blue." He held out his drawing triumphantly. "Look."

Gavin's rendering of the go-cart he wanted to build bore an unfortunate resemblance to his earlier drawing of the purple cat that was going to eat Prue.

She checked over Ryan's shoulder and sighed. His looked like a Formula One Car, sleek, gorgeous and completely unrealistic.

"What do you think?" he asked Gavin, presenting his drawing with flourish. Gavin took it and studied it, and then, tongue caught between his teeth began drawing furiously right on top of his father's carefully wrought lines.

Prue held her breath when he handed it back. Ryan's original drawing had been obliterated by a large purple blob.

But Ryan studied Gavin's alterations seriously, and declared them perfect.

"Now," Ryan said, "to begin. What do we need first?"

"Wheels," Gavin declared.

"Where do you suppose—"

Their eyes both lit on the pram parked in the corner of the nursery.

"You can't have that!" Prue said, but she found herself unceremoniously ignored, the two princes, father and son, grabbed the baby's pram, and chortling with gleeful, evil laughter they raced down the royal hallway with it.

"I've created a monster. Two monsters," Prue told the baby, but she was aware that wasn't how she felt at all. She had brought them together, given them something to focus on outside of themselves, but that still asked them to work as a team. With any luck, the rest would look after itself.

The courtyard below the nursery window became the hub of activity. Prue gave the father and son space, but watched from the upper window, laughing out loud when Ryan tried to burglarize the pram for parts. The pram was an unfortunately well-built piece of equipment and did not part with its parts at all willingly.

Finally one tire clattered off, and Ryan and Gavin high-fived happily!

Later, Prue brought them a snack of cookies and milk.

Three wheels were off the pram. Ryan's knuckles were skinned. She noticed the dark springy hair on his knuckles.

Hairy knuckles *and* his toe affliction! Those women at the bottom of the elevator needed to give themselves a shake. The man was seriously flawed. Still, Prue was shocked to discover she thought his hairy knuckles looked adorable. Horrible but adorable.

And maybe just a little sexy.

Before she let her mind go too far down that track, she drew her gaze away from the prince's hands and focused on Gavin, who was looking faintly worried that the crumpled drawing he was holding in a dirty small hand was not materializing a little more instantly.

"I hope you've arrived with more than cookies," Ryan told her in an undertone.

"I have," she whispered. "I've come with words of advice."

"Thank God."

She beckoned to him and he leaned close.

She whispered in his ear. "It's not about the go-cart. It's about Gavin. And you."

"Ahhh," he said, and he looked at her intently. It felt for all the world as if she was being seen for the first time. As if all her life she had been burdened with her perceived imperfections—red hair, impetuousness, temper, her equivalents to hairy knuckles and crooked teeth—and suddenly someone saw them not as imperfections at all.

Someone thought her yelling and shaking her fist was, well, adorable. Horrible and adorable, likely, just like hairy knuckles. And maybe, in unguarded moments, did he find her just a little sexy? He must! He *had* tried to kiss her.

She had to remind herself, sternly, not to go there. It was not about her. "So, what can I do to help?"

"I'm so glad you asked," Prince Ryan said.

* * *

Ryan knew he should feel guilty. He had tried to kiss a woman in his employ. It was completely inappropriate.

And yet, to think she was really any sort of employee didn't feel right, either. In very short order she had become the owner of his son's heart.

And very nearly the owner of his, too.

What would that kiss have told him about her? Probably, he realized ruefully, not nearly as much as leaving her with the pony had.

He had left her with that pony on purpose, knowing he would be entertained by her antics. He had beelined it for that upstairs window as soon as he had left her.

And he had not been disappointed. Watching her struggle with the headstrong, miniature equine, had been terribly enjoyable. The whole day—with the exception of having to change Miss Stinky Pants—had been amazingly enjoyable.

Until the moment Gavin had looked at him like Ryan kept a cellar full of the corpses of those he had killed personally!

But Prue seemed determined to wave her magic wand at that, too, and already the rawness of it was fading. If Gavin was afraid of him, it didn't show now as he hammered happily away at the remaining pram wheel.

Of course he was aware a gentleman would have gone and rescued her from the pony. That might have even been his original plan. He knew that pony was part Shetland and part flower fiend and part pure ornery devil.

But here was the strange truth: he had been raised to be a complete gentleman. He had opened doors and risen when a woman entered the room, and kissed extended hands since he was just a little older than Gavin. A damsel in distress really should have been right up his alley! And surely a pony pushing her into thorny bushes could have qualified her as a damsel in distress. But he was taking a perverse enjoyment in paying her back for her comments about his toes. There was nothing wrong with his toes!

Prudence had a gift for bringing the rogue out in him, a man who actually enjoyed having his toes found wanting, a fist shaken at him, that colorful Gaelic curse intended for the well-deserving pony extended to him. It was a novelty, and it was something more than a novelty.

He wondered if he should mention the near-miss-kiss to Gavin, to see if he could find out why his son had reacted so strongly. But when he shot a look at him, the boy seemed so contented, that Ryan decided to leave it for now.

It was way past Gavin's bedtime when Prue finally insisted they finish up, that it was over for the day. It had been a long day, but Ryan was still very, very sorry for it to end.

"I'll take him up," he said, aware of all the nights he had missed doing just that.

He saw Gavin hesitate.

"Good idea," Prue said. "Perhaps the two of you could discuss colors for your creation. And a name. Don't you think it should have a name?"

Gavin's hesitation disappeared. Ryan suspected she had known it would, and saw how cleverly she used diversion instead of confrontation. He made a quiet note of that strategy to add to his almost nonexistent parenting arsenal.

After he put Gavin to bed, he hoped he would see her. He hoped that maybe they could pick up where they had left off this afternoon—this time without the presence of the hostile witness. He might give her an opportunity to change her stubborn foolish mind about his toes!

But Prue was nowhere to be seen. And unless he was mistaken, over the next few days, she was very sure not to find herself alone with him.

He didn't know whether to be offended or amused. No woman had ever spurned his desire to kiss her before! In those heady days before he had married, it had seemed as though every girl in the world was in love with him.

And he, of course, with half of them. Was it just pure bad luck that he had ended up with the one who could not care about him? These days he took the adulation a lot less seriously. He was well aware he was not loved for himself, but for a stereotype as unattainable and as unreal as pots of gold at the end of the rainbow.

Prue seemed determined to see him in a realistic light, though.

In fact, she seemed delighted to extract her revenge for the pony incident. And she didn't have to lift a finger to do it! She watched, quietly gleeful, as he had hammered his thumb, said words he shouldn't be saying in front of his son, and tore a board off the cart and threw it into those already damaged flower gardens. She watched, and given how opinionated she could be on just about any subject, it was frustrating that she did not offer a single helpful suggestion as he had tried to figure out rudimentary steering and braking.

"I don't think that is going to work," could hardly be considered helpful. Neither could, "Where is the CD player?" Or "Hmm, how do I turn on the air-conditioning?"

Now, days after they had begun Prue, Gavin and Ryan, dotted with purple paint, stood looking at the finished product.

He was a man totally accustomed to success. Everything

he turned his hand was brilliantly successful. Prince Ryan Kaelan was and always had been a perfectionist.

And yet the go-cart was a disaster.

It had taken three days to get it to this point.

It bore absolutely no resemblance to his initial drawing. In fact it did not look like a car at all.

And yet, if it was a disaster, it was a joyous one. The days taken to create this could never be taken away from him. There was a place in him, sacred, where lived the laughter of his son, a grimy hand in his, purple paint on good shoes. There was a place in him, sacred, where his daughter played on a blanket, cooing and chortling, while he and Gavin worked side by side on their project. The road worthiness of the vehicle seemed secondary.

Prue had it just right when she had whispered to him, "It's not about the go-cart."

It was about taking the fear from his son's eyes, overcoming that underlying hostility he had felt from Gavin since the death of Raina. It was about them laughing together, working like a team, behaving like a father and son who knew each other, and better yet, liked one another.

Still, the cart itself, for all it had accomplished, was an astoundingly humble contraption. It looked like a large, crooked, very purple box perched precariously on pram wheels. It listed dangerously to one side.

The inside was even more primitive, except for the seat, which was an ordinary wooden kitchen chair that he and Gavin had pilfered when the cook wasn't looking. They'd sawed the legs off and bolted it to the frame. The steering wheel was an old cart wheel, too large, and the brakes were a pair of ski poles, shoved through holes in the floor of the cart.

He glanced at Gavin, dreading disappointment in his son's face.

But Gavin was looking at their creation with awe.

"It looks just like the box Prue drew on the airplane," he declared with satisfaction, as if that was how he had planned it all along.

"It does, doesn't it?" Ryan agreed. "Do you still wish the cat would eat her?"

"Oh, no, Dah, that was a long time ago."

To a small boy weeks were a long time, and yet to Ryan, too, it was almost impossible to imagine his life before she had come along. Silly, how the promise of this go-cart and spending time with his son—and her—filled him with eagerness for each day.

Royal business was going to hell in a handbasket, Ronald had told him, but looking at Gavin right now, Ryan thought maybe royal business, the tiny lad who would one day be king, had probably never been in better shape.

"I must drive it," Gavin declared.

"Of course you must," Prue said and ruffled his hair.

But as they pushed it over to a driveway with a small slope, Ryan had misgivings.

The cart was too rickety to put his son in. It had brought them together. It had served a purpose. If they never tested it—

Prudence laid her hand on his arm, and he looked at her, saw that she had the uncanny ability to know what he thought.

"Let him go," she said quietly.

"How do you do that? Know what I am thinking?"

She laughed. "It is not so hard to know what a father is thinking."

Not a prince. A father. Astonishing how he appreciated being seen as that first. "I can't let him get in that thing. He could be hurt."

"A scratch," she agreed, "or a bruise. Nothing life threatening. Better to be hurt than to live in a glass bubble where you can't be hurt at all."

And even though he knew she was talking about Gavin, and that she had not intended the statement to have any kind of double meaning, Ryan couldn't help but wonder if those rules applied to his own life.

Ryan had been hurt by the rejection of Raina, bruised by it, even though she had not ever allowed him to love her. How much worse would the pain be if you allowed yourself to love? Was he going to let past experiences stop him? Or was he going to take his scratches and bruises?

Now he felt regret, sharp and aching. The go-cart was done. The intensity of this time together, he and his son, and his daughter, and Prue, was finished. The business of Momhilegra badly needed his attention.

Ryan sighed, strapped a helmet to his son's head and put him in the seat of the cart. He gave last minute instructions about the braking system. He had no faith at all that the steering would work. What in his life had prepared him to build a steering system for a go-cart?

Prue could be wrong! She often was, though she was too pigheaded to ever admit it gracefully. His son was so small. He could break a bone, knock his teeth out. But Ryan bit back his fears. His son evidently had none when it came to the go-cart, and he did not want to be the one to introduce the evil weed of fear where it did not exist.

Gavin climbed into the car eagerly, his head listing as

badly as the car from the weight of the helmet. He experimented with the steering wheel, which he could barely turn, and the brakes.

Having completed his checklist, he settled into a chair that Ryan suddenly wished they had developed a seat belt for.

"Push," Gavin ordered.

Prue and Ryan put their shoulders behind the cart. It was remarkably heavy. It rolled, stopped, lurched, and stopped.

Prue laughed and her shoulder touched his, and Ryan felt stronger than he had ever felt. One more mighty push and the cart was careening down the hill, picking up speed, so much so that Ryan could not keep up with it.

"Brakes," he screamed at his son.

He was rewarded with a little shower of sparks shooting up behind the cart.

Unfortunately his son could not manipulate the brakes and steering at the same time, a design flaw Ryan had not considered, and the cart veered wildly to the left, and hit the curb that lined the driveway.

The right front wheel wobbled dangerously, but the cart, undeterred, leaped up over the curb and bumped over the grass. The wobbly tire flew off, the cart bounced, hit the nearest tree with a loud pop, and splintered into a million purple pieces.

Ryan heard an unearthly howling. He raced to the wreckage, fell to his knees and lifted his son from the debris. Gavin wrapped his arms around his father's neck.

And that's when Ryan realized the howling was laughter.

And warmth, like the first of the spring sun after a winter that had been too long and cold, touched him and spread through him.

Prue joined them on the grass, wrapped her arms around the pair of them, and covered Gavin's face with kisses. Apparently the state of Gavin's toes were not connected to the performance of her lips!

Ryan wished he could keep this moment forever: the scent of her hair, and crushed grass, the laughter in the air, the weight of his son in his arms.

But Prue broke away, and got up. She inspected the wreckage then gingerly lifted a piece of it with toe.

Beautiful toes, the pink nails showing through her open-toed sandals. "Can this be saved?"

Ryan got up, set Gavin down, brushed grass off his slacks. He looked at the heap of splinters. "I seriously, seriously doubt it," he said. He tried to sound unhappy, but nothing could be further from the truth.

Gavin came and stood beside him. "Dah, what are we going to do?"

The most important matters in his kingdom needed his attention. He felt as if, in the past, he might have been confused about what that was, but not any longer.

"We are going to build another one, of course." He lifted Gavin onto his shoulders, bent and retrieved the wheels, all that was salvageable.

"Okay," he said, "back to the drawing board."

CHAPTER EIGHT

"I CHRISTEN thee The Royal Cat," Gavin said, and gave his new go-cart a resounding whack with a plastic bottle. Then, grinning from ear to ear, he tipped the bottle, and poured sparkling lemonade over the front of his vehicle.

The name was written across the back in the large letters of his new ability to print.

Prue watched the happiness in his face and hugged herself, reviewed the last three weeks and added up the costs: twelve go-cart prototypes equaled three gallons of purple paint, two prams without wheels, and five garbage cans—complete with the Royal crest—full of splintered wood and bent ski poles.

Three weeks added up to three sunburned noses, even with the two bottles of sunscreen, sixteen picnic lunches, four gallons of Kool-Aid, twelve stinky diaper changes (by the prince), free purple hair streaking for all, including the baby, four broken fingernails (for her), and more ruined clothes than she could keep track of.

Three weeks added up to five days that had been warm enough that Prince Ryan had taken his shirt off, one that he had taunted her by wearing open-toed sandals, three days where the project moved into the royal dining room because of rain.

Three weeks added up to her being at the receiving end (from Prince Ryan) of twenty-one aggravated frowns, sixty-three half smiles, twelve winks, thirty-two shoulder brushings, six times his hand had lingered in hers just a little longer than it should have after she'd passed him the paintbrush, a dozen looks that would have to be considered smoldering, and three times when he might have kissed her but she pulled back at the last possible second.

Every royal engagement for days had been canceled or rescheduled and tonight was no exception. Prince Ryan should have been at Mollywog, the biggest hotel in Morun, welcoming the visiting dignitaries for tomorrow's Thirty-first Annual Soap Box Derby. But Ryan had learned the fine art of delegation, and his cousin, Milford Kaelan, a duke who was young and handsome and fun—not anything as stuffy as his title suggested—was having the time of his life filling in at the royal functions.

It was getting dark and it was past Gavin's bedtime, again, but this was the moment they had all been working for and waiting for.

Gavin, to great cheering from Ryan and Prue climbed into the newest model of The Royal Cat, and set it in motion down the hill. There were no crashes, no drama. The cart, slightly more sleek than the first model, and certainly far more road-worthy, trundled down the driveway at no great speed, and ran out of momentum very shortly after running out of hill.

"An anticlimatic moment if I've ever had one," Ryan said to her.

"I know what you mean."

"I'm sorry it's over."

"Me, too."

Not that it was over. The race was tomorrow! But all the best parts did seem to be over!

"Prue, would you like to attend the Derby ball tomorrow night?" Ryan hesitated. "With me?"

So far it had been so safe, the three of them, or when the baby was there, the four of them. But sometimes it was too easy to forget *why* she had started this, solely for the children.

Because it felt as if it had been for her. It felt as if her time on Momhilegra had healed something in her that all her frantic kissing of toads had not even come close to touching.

But a ball? With the prince? Would there be a pumpkin turned into a carriage and a glass slipper? Because truly she felt like Cinderella.

But then reality hit her.

"Tomorrow? Ryan! I have purple paint in my hair. And nothing to wear! You snake."

"I appreciate the invitation, Your Royal Highness," he coached her dryly. "Of course I will go with you. I can't think of anything I'd like better."

"Now—" she wagged her finger at him "—you're being arrogant."

"An arrogant snake. Did you know I was voted as one of *People* magazine's sexiest bachelors last year?"

"You must have kept your toes hidden."

"Just say yes or no for God's sake Prue, or I'll—"

"What?" she asked.

"You're getting that mulish look on your face," he said and she amended her list. Sixty-four half smiles.

"Say yes, or you'll what?" she said *mulishly* just so that

he'd never guess that sometime, somewhere, she had quite fallen in love with the way those two front teeth overlapped ever so slightly.

"Paint the pony purple," he threatened.

"And that would bother me why?"

"Because your name would be what I was painting. Right across his stubborn little ass."

"Okay," she said, "I'll go. Since you've threatened me. You'll have to put Gavin to bed, though. I have things to do. Hair repair. And a gown at this time of night. I can't believe you'd do this to me."

He watched her go up the hill, and smiled. A million women in the world would fall over themselves backward to say yes to him.

Thank God he had found the one who wouldn't. Not in a million years. He had never seen her look more beautiful: hot, sweaty, her hair everywhere, her legs long and sleek and beginning to brown from all the days in the sun. She had the American girl thing: she wore shorts, and he was so glad.

He was stunned by what he suddenly knew.

She had done just as her name had warned him she would do.

Win slow.

She had won him slow. His heart filled when he looked after her. His life felt complete in ways it never had before, even though he was the prince of the most special place in the world.

Maybe the most special place in the world had nothing to do with Momhilegra. Maybe it had to do with that place in a man's heart, that place he discovered when he least expected it.

That place called love.

When he thought of that word in the context of Prue, it was like everything in him softened. It was like the colors melted into a pallet of pastel around him, and like the air turned into an embrace. He could suddenly smell the imported magnolias and lilacs that bloomed on the hill, he could feel something within himself he had never felt before.

"Dah." Gavin was coming up the hill, panting with exertion, pulling his cart on the string they had attached to the front of it. "Do you think I might win tomorrow?" he asked eagerly.

"We already have," Ryan said. "Come on. Let's go get your pajamas on. No story, though. It's late, and you need to be rested for the big race."

The next day the island was crazy. There was nothing the people of Momhilegra loved so much as having fun. Most of the major roads were closed, the larger hills blocked off for the different categories of races. Pubs were overflowing and bands playing.

Ryan had to open the festivities, but as soon as he was done, he donned a baseball cap and sunglasses so he could—with the help of two burly bodyguards—push through the crowds without being stopped for chats or autographs to get to the children's hill for Gavin's race, which was the first race of the day.

Prue was watching anxiously for him and she waved, recognizing him somehow even with his disguise.

"I see you got the purple out of your hair," he said.

"Never mind my hair. I'm so excited for Gavin. And so worried about him. His hopes are so high! And the crowd loves him. How can he handle that kind of pressure, especially if he loses? Everyone is so focused on him."

Her love for his child shone out of her, and it felt like the most extraordinary gift that the woman he loved so much loved his son with all her heart. But did that feeling extend to the father?

"Pushers, to your stations."

"You go," she said. "It's your moment. Yours and his."

It was *their* moment, but since he knew a throng of thousands would not prevent her from arguing with him, he took up his place behind The Royal Cat. He took off his ball cap and the sunglasses.

The crowd recognized him instantly and roared their approval. Gavin grinned and waved. The starting horn blared and Ryan pushed with all his might to the red line where the pusher was required to let go.

They were off.

Prue came and stood beside him. "Go, Gavin," she shrieked. She was jumping up and down and clapping, irrepressible. He found himself shouting, too.

Two of the carts collided almost instantly, and another one raced off course and the spectators had to leap out of the way.

That left only five carts in the running. Gavin's ran a steady fourth the whole way down the hill.

But Gavin got out, past the finish line and was jumping around with his hands over his head as though he had won. As was every other little person in his category, including a little girl in a pink dress.

Ryan was asked to give out the awards, and to his delight there was a trophy for each child. He made a particular fuss over the three children whose misadventures had kept them from completing the race. Gavin got "Most Innovative." He was thrilled, even though on the way home later that day, after watching as many of the races as they could, and eating cotton candy until they were nearly sick, he admitted he didn't know what that meant.

"It means your cart had the most imagination go into it." Prue told him.

"Oh," Gavin said tiredly. "I don't know about that but it had the most fun, didn't it, Prue?"

"It did," she said. "Now I have to go get ready for the ball."

"The ball?" Gavin said suspiciously.

"I'm going dancing with your father."

Remembering Gavin's reaction to the near kiss at the pond, both of them had been very, very careful to keep the growing attraction between them under wraps.

Now, Ryan saw, gratefully, that she was slowly introducing Gavin to the idea that the adults were going to have a life separate from their involvement with him.

Gavin contemplated that for a moment, then shrugged. "Come kiss me good-night before you go," he said.

And so Ryan was reading Gavin his bedtime story when Prue swept into the room. Ryan got up off the bed, and the book fell to the floor.

Nothing could have prepared him for Prue like this.

She was in a strapless green gown that shimmered as if it had been infused with moonlight. A lace shawl hid her naked shoulders, but the bodice hugged her every delightful curve. The skirt flared out from the waist, yards of material sweeping the floor around her.

Her hair was up—really up, not falling out of a haphazard bun, and it made the bone structure of her face amazing. She had done something with her eyes—or maybe it was the reflection off the dress—but they had never seemed so hauntingly green to him, so sensual. And her lips! They were the color of rubies, full and inviting. She gave just the smallest hint she was nervous when she licked them.

Like a man in a dream, he crossed the floor to her, and held out both his hands.

She took them, her grasp tentative, and her eyes never left his.

"Look at you," he croaked, like a commoner who had just been presented to royalty. He leaned toward her. Finally he could wait no longer. He had to taste her. He had to know something that her kiss would tell him.

But before it happened, Gavin bolted from the bed and his sturdy body was thrust between them.

"Don't you dare kiss her," Gavin screamed. "You will kill her just like you did my mother."

Shocked, he dropped his hands from Prue's, and stared at his son. Gavin met his gaze, then hurtled a furious *I hate you.* Crying, he turned and ran away.

Gavin believed Ryan had killed his mother?

He thought if he listened very hard at this moment Prince Ryan Kaelan would hear the sound of his own heart breaking in two.

Prue felt the quickness with which the mood in the room had altered was cruel.

Ryan dropped her hands, and shook his head, like a boxer who had just been surprised by a hard punch. "Why do I feel like it just took me two seconds to lose everything it took me so long to gain? How can he not know how I love him? How can I have failed him so drastically?" And then more softly, "How can my own son believe I killed his mother?"

"He's five, Ryan," she said, keeping her voice low and reassuring, despite the fact she, too, was upset. "He's very articulate for five. I think that has made us all think we are dealing with a small adult. But Gavin's reasoning skills are not near developed. His ability to separate reality and fantasy are not in place yet."

And she would know all about that! Maybe that's what had happened to her—her development arrested at the time of her mother's death. Maybe that's why she was able to feel such kinship with Gavin from the start.

Ryan was not hearing her. She was not getting through to him.

Prue moved in closer to him, until the skirt of her dress was touching his leg. She laid her hand on her arm. But touching him did not feel casual. It felt as if she *needed* to touch him, as if her touch could tell him something.

In his face was such terrible sadness, defeat, loneliness.

"You shouldn't look at it that way," she said. "You've finally gotten to the bottom of why he's so angry with you. That's good."

But she could see Ryan was not convinced, that her touch was not breaking down the barrier going up around him.

It seemed to her that everything she had seen happen in the last magic month was about to slip away, too.

It seemed like he would go now—back to a world where everything was safer, and where his heart didn't have to be open to the barbed arrows of one too young to know the hurt he could cause.

Ryan looked off into the distance, and she saw everything he was in his eyes. She saw the burdens he carried and the loneliness. But she also saw his strength, and his discipline and the goodness that was at the core of his heart.

And she wanted him to know he did not deserve to be lonely.

She wanted him to know there was a place he could lay those burdens down.

Above all, she wanted him to know he was a man who could be loved. Not by adoring throngs, who did not know the first thing about who he really was, but by those close to him. Those he needed to love him.

She wanted him to know, but she could see words would not penetrate the cloak of defensiveness he was drawing around himself.

Without thinking, she rose on her toes, and took his lips with her own.

His lips tasted of wild raspberry wine, of wisps of clouds, of ocean spray breaking over rocks. His lips tasted of the whole world: of every dream she had ever held for herself, and of every good thing she had ever experienced.

In that kiss was all: joy, sorrow, completeness, life and death and rebirth.

She had kissed a prince. She had kissed him even knowing all his flaws. She had kissed him knowing he had hair growing on his knuckles, and the world's worst toes, and that he hid in remoteness, and that he could be frightfully arrogant without even knowing that he was being that way. She had kissed him knowing full well Prince Ryan Kaelan was not the man without fault that his subjects wanted to believe he was.

She had kissed a prince, and he had not become a toad.

He had become a man.

A man who needed her to love him.

She staggered back from him, stunned at the truth she had found in that kiss.

"I need to go find Gavin," she stammered. She needed to be away from what she had just discovered.

She foolishly, heedlessly recklessly had fallen in love with the prince.

"No," he said, and this time he touched her arm, and she saw that kiss had accomplished exactly what she wanted. It had spoken the language of the heart, and he had heard its message.

"No," he said, "I need to go talk to Gavin."

She nodded, still off balance.

"We can still go to the ball," Ryan said. "If you want to. After I talk to Gavin."

But it was obvious his heart was not in it. And neither was hers.

"I don't really feel like it," she said. Prudence Winslow did not feel like going to the ball. With a prince. Life could be so cruel.

He touched her lips with his thumb, and said softly. "Will you meet me? In my apartment?"

She backed away from his touch, as confused as she had ever been. "I—I—I don't know." How could she experience a kiss like that, and not nearly die for wanting it again? Is that why he was inviting her to his apartment? Had she opened a door behind which were things frightening and complex? That kiss had told him she loved him! She was certain of it!

How had things gone so terribly wrong when she had been trying so hard to make them right?

"I want to let you know how my meeting with Gavin goes," he said quietly.

"Oh." So, it was not about the kiss, then. Of course it wasn't. Women threw themselves at the prince all the time. Idelle had informed her they threw their undergarments at him.

He wanted to go to his apartment so they could discuss

Gavin privately. No doubt he wanted to bring the relationship between him and her back to where it needed to be. The professional and the personal had become so intermingled in the last weeks.

She had forgotten she was the hired help. She had forgotten her place. *But he'd invited her to the ball!* But that was before she'd revealed to him, with that impulsive kiss, that she was not going to be able to accept a date lightly!

"Yes, of course," she said.

"Nine," he said.

It sounded suspiciously like a command.

But that was what she needed to remember: despite the fact they had laughed together, and painted a go-cart purple together, despite the fact she had seen him nearly naked, and helped him learn to change a diaper, and despite the fact he had asked her to the ball, he was her employer. Not her friend.

Certainly not her potential lover even though that kiss had opened that door and now she was not at all sure she had the strength to wrestle it shut again!

Her stomach did a somersault at the very thought. Good grief! Where in the book of Royal Protocol did it discuss that? Protocol for lovers?

She could not be his lover! She was his son's nanny. That would only hurt and confuse the child in the end. It could only hurt and confuse everyone involved.

Prince Ryan knew that. And she knew that. Why hadn't she thought through those things before she's said yes to his invitation to the ball? Before she'd scrambled around frantically finding this dress?

Because she didn't think straight around him, that's why! From the very first he had completely addled her!

When she went to say good-night to Gavin, Idelle said he was already sleeping. "He's tuckered right out," Idelle said. "His father was with him for the longest time. They both seemed exhausted."

Prudence went in to see Gavin anyway, brushed that thatch of dark hair from his forehead, reminded herself her first responsibility was to him. She could not do anything that might hurt him. She could not do anything that even had the *potential* to harm.

She smiled at that. Her vow had really worked after all. Because up until she had taken it, she had never been able to put anyone's needs ahead of her own.

And now the thought of not putting this helpless little boy's needs ahead of her own was repugnant to her.

She arrived at the prince's door right at nine determined to be businesslike, though if that was really her intention she probably would have taken off the dress, and she had been enormously reluctant to do that. She wanted him to see her as beautiful, a woman worthy of attending a ball with him. But what were the repercussions of being seen publically with the prince? Had he thought that through before he had asked her?

His apartment was no surprise—the same kind of heavy furnishings that had been so evident in the nursery and the children's bedrooms until she had gotten in there.

"Everything in here looks about a million years old," she said, trying to make conversation.

"Well, that's appropriate," he said. "Because that's how old I feel."

Something in his voice calmed the chaos of her thoughts. She forgot all about her turmoil, her preoccupation with looking beautiful.

His face did look like he'd aged!

"That poor kid," he said. "He's been carrying that burden for a year. Since his mother died. Thinking he knew a big secret."

He gave her a glass of wine without asking if she wanted one, and took his own over to the couch. He waited for her to sit down.

She took a cautious sip of the wine. She was not sure she should be adding wine to the potent mix already in the room, but it was delicious. She took another long sip. He sat down beside her.

"You are not going to believe this," he said.

Something in her heart became very tender. He was not treating her like an employee, not even a trusted one. His tone of voice was one that was reserved for friends, for equals, for the people you trusted most in the world.

Dare she hope loved most in the world?

"Gavin overheard things. You know how smart he is, but he put the things he'd overheard with the things he thought he knew, and he came up with the most impossible conclusion."

She took another sip of her wine.

"Gavin thought when I kissed his mother it planted a seed in her." He grinned ruefully. "As she grew fatter—his words not mine—he thought it must have been a pumpkin seed, also his words not mine. Sometime, he's not sure how, the pumpkin turned into a baby. Sara. I'm assuming he couldn't cope with the thought someone as small and sweet and helpless as his little sister killed his mother, and so the responsibility became mine. Because I planted the seed."

"And so when it looked as though I might kiss you that day by the pond, and again today, he thought I would kill you, too."

"Ryan, that poor little boy!"

"I know. I told him what had really happened as best I could. I'm not sure I did a very good job of it—it's very hard to explain why a young woman in the prime of her life would die, but I know he wanted to believe it was not my fault. Or his. Or anyone's. I think it will take some time, but I think his heart knows the truth."

"I'll help in anyway I can," she said.

"In a very short time, Prudence, you have come to mean the world to my son."

He hesitated and took a sip of his own wine, set it down. "And to me," he said in a low voice. "Prudence, I think you should marry me."

She stared at him. Here she was thinking he was going to put some much needed professional distance between them, and he was proposing?

Oh, he was the most infuriating man! No courtship? No flowers? No romance?

She meant a lot to his son, so they should get married? Oh!

She looked around for something to throw at him! She had finally had the kiss of her dreams and he had turned into a toad on the installment method?

She was going to show him there was a little more to this than meaning the world to each other. Why the cretin now seemed to be totally unaware she was in the world's sexiest gown. But, why throw things? There was a much better way of dealing with this.

So, she leaned back, and took a sip of her wine. The glass was nearly gone, but she needed its courage! She blinked at him.

"Is it warm in here?" she asked throatily.

"No."

"Oh." She tossed the shawl off her dress, revealing the full drama of the neckline. She fanned herself. "I'm finding it quite warm. Perhaps it's the wine."

"Let me open a window," he said hastily, trying to look everywhere but at her neckline!

He got up, and she reached for him. She had planned the move of a seductress, but somehow it didn't turn out that way. She managed to grab him a little too hard. It wasn't quite the romantic move she'd had in mind. He fell and sprawled awkwardly on top of her.

She could feel his masculine strength, and the beating of his heart.

"Well, well, well," he said, looking at her gravely.

He was supposed to be out of control by now! They were pressed intimately together. She was trying to tempt the prince to ravage her. So that she could find all kinds of flaws when he kissed her again!

He made the mistake of trying to scramble to his feet!

She tangled her hands around his neck and pulled him to her. She took his lips in hers, determined that this time she really would find a toad. She hoped he had bad breath. She hoped he got spit on her. She hoped his kiss made her feel nauseous.

Instead it happened all over again.

She melted. His kiss took her to worlds she had begun to think only existed in dreams. It felt as if the stars were coming out over an inky sea, as if she was soaring up there with them, in the heavens.

This was backfiring badly on her.

She shoved him off of her, got up shakily, adjusted her gown.

"I wouldn't—" She closed her eyes and gathered all her strength. "I wouldn't marry you if you were the last person on earth."

She thought of throwing the few remaining drops of her wine on him, but that seemed altogether too passionate, the gesture of someone who cared, someone who was wounded.

A little smile tickled across his lips, and her knuckles tightened on the wineglass stem.

"What have I done to upset you?"

"You sincerely don't know?"

"No. Prudence? Could you put down the wineglass? You are making me very nervous."

Deliberately, she set it down.

"Prince Ryan Kaelan," she said, "I want you to know that is the shoddiest marriage proposal I ever heard!"

She stormed from the room, almost knocking over poor Ronald who was coming down the hall with a silver tray, the most delectable aromas wafting out from under it.

He stopped, and looked at her face. Resigned, he handed her the tray. "I take it you'll be having this to go?"

"Thank you," she said and took it, even though she'd had no idea Ryan was planning supper, and even though she was not the least bit hungry. Let Ryan the High and Mighty starve. That should give him something to think about.

Imagine asking a woman to marry you because you thought highly of her! Because your child got on well with her!

"Did you throw anything at him?" Ronald asked in an undertone.

"I wouldn't give him the satisfaction."

"Oh." Ronald sounded unabashedly disappointed.

* * *

Well, Ryan thought, that had gone badly. Ronald came in looking slightly guilty.

"I'm afraid I gave her the dinner, sir."

"I've lost my appetite."

When she had kissed him this afternoon it had felt as if the light had gone on in a world that had known nothing but darkness. It felt as if seeds planted a long time ago in cold soil had felt the warmth and begun to grow.

Grow flowers of hope and expectation.

It had seemed, from what he had read in her lips, that she loved him. And he had known for some time that he loved her.

So wasn't the practical thing to do to get married?

He didn't realize he had been thinking out loud until Ronald cleared his throat. "Most young ladies don't think of marriage as a practical thing," he suggested.

Of course not, Ryan realized. He had to woo her, the same way as he'd had to woo her to get her to work here.

Only it wasn't the same thing this time. It wasn't about winning! He didn't want to feel like he was manipulating her. He didn't want to feel like he was trying to win her over against her will.

He wanted her to love him willingly. To be his wife willingly.

He thought of the fire in her eyes after his clumsy proposal. Okay, it had been clumsy, completely unworthy of her.

But what did he know about such things? He'd never even had to ask a girl on a date. These things were looked after for him.

She'd very nearly thrown that wineglass. He could feel a smile starting in him at the thought. And then it died. Is that how he wanted to spend his life? Ducking wineglasses? Life with her would be more like *Taming of the Prue*, than *The Sound of Music*!

Yes. It was how he wanted to spend his life. Ducking wineglasses would be so much nicer than what he had with Gavin and Sara's mother.

A chasm between them that couldn't be crossed. She had loved another. She had done what was expected of her.

But it had killed something in her. The part of her, that perhaps, given time, could have loved him. She acted as though her marriage was a prison term, and nothing he could do or say ever made it up to her.

He had not made her say yes!

But feeling what he had felt now, he wished he would have said no. He wished he would have set her free.

But if you took back time, did you take back his two beautiful children, too?

Was this love then? One minute you felt like your head was bursting, and the next you felt like laughing? You began to look at your life differently? Evaluating from a different place? Coming up shorter than you had hoped?

Would Gavin have ever reached the erroneous conclusion that Ryan had killed his mother, if he had been assured there was love between them?

Ryan did not like roller coasters!

He could not change the past, but he could vow to try to be a better man. One who knew his own heart and was true to it.

He preferred a nice sedate ride in a carriage to a roller coaster. Should he woo Prue? With flowers and wine and chocolate? Maybe with a ride in a horse drawn carriage. Would that be romantic? Or manipulative?

She'd probably throw horse pukey at him.

"A chance you'll have to take, sir," Ronald said cheerfully.

Ryan glared at him. Ronald seemed inordinately pleased to find his master in this state of upset.

CHAPTER NINE

THE next morning Prue walked through a small gate in a stone wall into a magnificent garden, but she barely noticed the beauty of the small space.

She was in love with Prince Ryan Kaelan. And she was in a predicament. She knew she should go from this island. She felt that Ryan needed to develop his own relationship with Gavin now. It was just as Mrs. Hilroy had said—oh, that seemed like so very long ago—she wanted her child to cry when she—not the nanny left the house.

That's what they deserved, Ryan and Gavin, a true father/son relationship. They knew how to do it now. Ryan knew how to do it.

There would be more go-carts for them to build. Birdhouses. Tree forts. There were so many places the two of them could explore on this island, seaside coves and deep forest retreats. Gavin would grow up learning how to ride horses, and drive pony traps. In time, when Sara was old enough, she would join the family activities with her father and her brother.

The thought of missing those moments filled Prue with grief that rivaled what she had felt when her father had died.

But how could she leave Gavin? He had lost his mother. He had thought he had no father he could trust. He had clung to her like a shipwreck survivor who had a life raft drift by. If she left now, he would only see it as abandonment.

And Sara! To miss her first steps and her first words, and her first day of school! She was probably going to be the first female Derby winner on Momhilegra!

Prue turned as the gate to this beautiful walled garden opened. When the queen walked in, dressed in what appeared to be a housecoat, she realized she had trespassed on a private space.

Prue curtsied awkwardly, very aware her jeans were frayed and her T-shirt old. "Your Majesty," she said. "I'm so sorry. This must be your personal garden. I didn't mean to—"

"Hush, dear." The woman came over to her.

Prudence tried to remember her protocol. If she offered her hand, take it. Her Majesty for the first address, and then ma'am after that. Her eyes slid, longingly to the gate of the garden.

But the most astonishing thing happened, the queen touched her cheek, and then looked at her own fingertips.

"My dear, you are crying," she said, distressed.

People were not allowed to casually touch the queen. It was in the book! But the queen had touched her. Ronald was probably lurking somewhere waiting to chastise Prudence for putting the monarch in this predicament.

"Over nothing," Prue assured her hastily, "I must—"

"You must come sit down," Queen Mayra said firmly, and led her to a bench. She heard Ryan in the voice, a woman very accustomed, as was he, of having her own way. Prue sat, and the queen sat beside her.

"I've never seen so many hummingbirds! It's such a lovely garden," Prue said, searching awkwardly for something to say.

"Pony-proof," the queen said dryly.

"Oh, dear. I'm so sorry."

"Nonsense. I watched it all from my window. It was one of those days I wasn't well enough to get out. It perked me up immeasurably."

"What's wrong with you?" Prue asked though she was sure that wasn't in the protocol book to ask such a terribly personal question of the queen.

"I have cancer." It was said bluntly, and with no self-pity.

"Oh, no!" Considering how little she knew this woman, Prue's regret was real and strong. Poor little Gavin!

"Another loss for Gavin," Queen Mayra said, watching Prue closely, as if she knew darn well Prue had been contemplating that very thing only a moment ago.

"And for Ryan," Prue said sadly, and then blushed at her slip. "I meant Prince Ryan, of course."

"Of course," the queen said, and then sighed. "A woman in my position really only wants one thing in the end. I would like for my child, my only son, to be happy."

"But he is!" Prue said.

"Yes. Since you came. I'm not sure I have ever seen this place—or Ryan—quite so brimming with activity and animation." She shook her head and smiled. "The go-cart was a marvel."

"Oh, it wasn't really," Prue said. "It was quite an awful go-cart."

"Well, you and I both knew from the beginning it wasn't about the go-cart. So, perhaps more even than a marvel."

Prue smiled.

"When Gavin came last night and showed me his trophy," Queen Mayra said, "it was a miracle. He was so pleased with himself, so healthy looking from all his days in the sun, so happy."

"He came in fourth," Prue said, thinking Gavin must have seen his grandmother before the other events of the evening.

"It's a measure of how good you are with him, that he had absolutely no idea whether he was first, fourth or dead last."

"Ryan's responsible for that attitude, I think. I mean Prince Ryan."

"Prudence—may I call you that?"

"Of course."

"I have limited energy. I'm afraid I have no time for small talk."

Prue shot up. "I'm sorry. Of course, I'll leave at once."

"Sit down," the queen snapped.

Prue sat. "Yes, ma'am."

"I want to know this…do you love my son?"

Prue stared at her. Her mouth worked. She wanted to say no, to keep her secrets to herself, but she could not lie to a dying woman.

"Yes," she whispered.

The queen tilted her head back, so that the sun touched it. She closed her eyes. A smile, soft and sweet, tickled the edges of her mouth.

"I know I'm desperately unsuitable," Prue said. "Believe me, I tried not to fall for him. I had taken a vow, you see, I had sworn off love, for one year."

The queen opened her eyes, and her hand found Prue's. "Tell me about it," she said, "This vow you made."

"You might think it's small talk!" Prue protested.

"Let me decide that."

Prue was not so sure she should be holding the queen's

hand, and yet despite that woman's obvious illness, she could feel strength there, and see compassion in those eyes that were as blue as Ryan's own. Suddenly words were spilling out of her like water, too long held, spilling over a dam.

"When I was a little girl," Prue said, rushing, trying not to take up too much time, "my mother died. And I don't know if my father was so torn up with grief over her, or if he'd always been that way, but he threw himself into his business. I was sent off to schools, I rarely saw him, when I did see him, I got the sense I was a big nuisance. I developed this longing for love—"

"Understandable," the queen said, and squeezed her hand so encouragingly that Prue took a deep breath and slowed down.

"I read books and watched movies and daydreamed of a man who would love me and the home we would have and what that would *feel* like. I cut pictures out from magazines of handsome men and beautiful houses, and golden retrievers and babies.

"When I was fourteen, I started dating."

"Much too young," the queen said disapprovingly, and in that statement Prue longed for the mother who had not been there to guide her.

"And every boy, and later every man that I dated, would get woven into my fantasy. I would dream of walking hand in hand, and candlelight dinners and even—" she blushed at the silliness of it "—horseback rides in moonlight, or swims in the darkness." She left out the skinny-dipping part of that fantasy, even though she had the awful feeling the queen might have guessed.

"I would imagine him giving me rings, on bended knee, and writing me poems. I would search for romantic little gifts to manipulate him to love me."

"Truly, I'm amazed no one did," the queen said.

"Well," Prue wailed, "some of them might have. But I had this final test they had to pass before we marched together into happily-ever-after—or anything else, if you know what I mean. I was convinced I would know the right one as soon as he kissed me. My one and only. The perfect man."

"Your prince," Queen Mayra said just a touch dryly.

"Yes," Prue said with a sigh. "My prince. Usually I knew, though, even before I kissed them that they were all wrong for the job. I found fault with everyone. I had a list. My Fatal Flaws List. Now I wonder if it wasn't because I felt so flawed myself. But I kept hoping I would find the one. But I didn't.

"Queen Mayra, I have kissed a thousand toads and not one of them has turned into a prince!"

The queen laughed, delighted.

"Then my father died last year, and it was like I had a moment of total clarity. I realized I was really only trying to get the love I had wanted from him. He was dead. So I gave it up. It was going very well, too. I discovered I loved children. I loved helping people. I had never known that before.

"And then I kissed your son," Prudence admitted. "I broke my vow to myself and kissed your son."

The garden got very quiet. Prudence could hear the song of the hummingbirds' wings at the feeder. She could hear a bumblebee and the sound of her own breathing.

"And?"

Prudence met Queen Mayra's eyes and looked away. "He's flawed!" she said desperately. "He's arrogant and bossy, and too used of getting his own way. He has crooked teeth and hairy knuckles and terrible, terrible toes."

"Well, not much chance of him getting bigheaded around you. Easy enough for a man in his position to do."

"I mean of course I found him attractive, just flawed. To be honest I always thought a blond man would be *the* one. Strawberry-blond babies. But Ryan is very dark and we would probably make ugly babies!"

She thought the queen should at least reprimand her about talking about the prince that way, but the queen said absolutely nothing, and into the silence Prue heard her own voice fall, each word like a gentle drop of rain bringing life to a parched land.

"And it didn't matter," she spoke her realization slowly. "It didn't matter that Ryan had flaws. I felt the way I had only dared to feel in my dreams when I kissed Ryan."

"And," the queen said mildly, "there is no such thing as an ugly baby. Really, Prue!"

"I just didn't want anyone cursed with my red hair."

The queen smiled and touched Prue's hair with a certain tolerant tenderness, then withdrew her hand. "I have something to say to you. Please listen carefully for they feel like the most important words I will ever speak."

The queen looked at her sternly. "You have been like Perceval pursuing the Holy Grail. You have been shouting, *How can the grail—love—serve me?* But love does not serve people. It is served. And so when you developed the maturity and depth of character to begin asking, *How may I serve the Grail—love—* then you became worthy of what you have always sought."

Maturity, depth of character? Prue was not sure she had either of those.

"When Ryan hired you, he told me about you saving the little boy from the car."

"It was nothing," Prue said.

"Of course it was something," the queen said a trifle impatiently. "It was a turning point. You became worthy of the holy thing you sought."

Prue felt her eyes tearing over. She had to bite down hard on her fist.

She recognized the truth of what the queen was saying. In a life that had been all about her, where she had scrabbled frantically to try to get her insatiable needs met, she had, for a few stopped seconds in time, been able to put Brian Hilroy's life ahead of her own. Because, simply, she had loved the child.

And when she had finally kissed Ryan, it had not been a kiss that sought. It had not sought a happy ending to her fairy tale, it had not sought to make her feel treasured or cherished or like a princess.

That kiss had sought to give rather than take.

And it was then, and only then, Prudence Winslow had finally felt everything, every single thing, that she had ever wanted to feel from a kiss.

"Ryan, too, is worthy," the queen said. "His life has demanded much of him. He has made huge personal sacrifices. And he has never complained or flinched from his duty.

"My son, like you, is worthy of the holiest of grails. That grail is love."

"He proposed to me," Prue admitted.

"He did?" the queen asked with interest.

"It went badly. I shouted at him! I told him it was a shoddy proposal if I'd ever heard one."

"And was it?"

"I don't think," Prue realized, "the shoddiness of the proposal had anything to do with my reaction. I'm so afraid."

"Tell me what you are afraid of."

"All those years," Prue said with wonder, "of picking people apart and finding their flaws, it was never about finding the perfect man. It was about *not* finding him. Because I was so afraid.

"I knew the real test wasn't in a kiss. I was afraid if anyone ever got to really know me they wouldn't love me, because my own father had not. I made sure I lost interest in them first."

"Ah," the queen said, pleased at Prue's conclusions.

"There's more! I knew the real test was in loving someone day in and day out. Loving them if they have the flu, or wake up crabby. Loving them when they get busy and distracted, and the family comes last. Loving them for them, instead of for me!"

The queen drew Prue to her, guided her head onto her shoulder and let her cry.

"You don't have to be afraid anymore," she said softly. "Come home, Prudence."

Home.

Her heart had recognized this unforgettable island as her home from the first moment she had set foot on it. Her heart had recognized those children as its children. Her heart had known Ryan would be the one, from the first moment her eyes had met the blue of his.

Her heart sighed against this woman who would be her mother.

Prue shot up from the chair. "I have to find him. I shouted at him. Oh, I have behaved badly."

"It's the red hair," the queen said, but not at all unkindly. She stood up, took Prue's face between both her hands and kissed both her cheeks. "Did you know if you arrange the letters of your name differently they spell Pure, not Prue?"

"Oh," Prue said softly, delighted.

"You have a pure heart, my dear child."

"Thank you," Prue said, trying very hard not to cry anymore.

"My son goes to a place when he has suffered a disappointment."

She didn't have to say anything more. Prue knew exactly that place, and her feet were already running toward it.

Ryan pulled himself from the icy water below Myria Falls. It was not an easy thing for a man to say the words, *I was wrong,* but this time he was wrong, and Prue was right, absolutely one hundred percent correct.

It had been a shoddy proposal. A cowardly proposal. It had been the proposal of a man who had been rejected emotionally by his own wife for six years. He had deliberately played it down, made it seem like it was about the children, about Gavin's well-being. Ryan had wanted to seem like he didn't care whether she accepted, one way or the other.

He had proposed badly because he was terrified of more rejection.

But here in this place of thundering falls and rainbows, the prince considered each of the suggestions Ronald had given him, added some of his own and formulated a careful and concise plan.

But it had to begin here, in this very place. He needed to, symbolically, pick up each of the dreams he had left here, each part of himself that he had abandoned, and put those things back in his heart. He had to be willing to risk all for what he wanted.

A woman like Prue required everything a man had to give. There was no room for fear or cowardice. He had to declare himself in no uncertain terms. She had to know the truth. He had to be his most vulnerable. He would die without her. Maybe not physically, but all that was best about him would die if he could not walk the days of his life with Prudence beside him.

And when a man was in that position, where he was contemplating the death of his own spirit, he had to be prepared to fight for what he wanted. He had to be prepared to storm the gates. He had to be prepared to bare all, risk all and be all that he could ever be.

He heard Prue coming and slipped quietly into the trees, and watched her. He thought she was probably looking for him, but he was doing this his way.

Quite possibly the rest of his life was going to be her way, so this would be his way.

Prue had gone to the falls. She had been so certain Ryan would be there, but he had not been. When she got back to the castle, she had tracked down Ronald but he claimed not to know where Ryan was. She saw a twinkle in his eye that said he did, but he refused to be cajoled out of his secret!

Idelle had taken Gavin and Sara to have the afternoon with their grandmother, and in her quarters Prue paced restlessly, as lonely as she had ever been.

And then she heard a little pinging at the window. Rain? Thank goodness the Derby had been yesterday. The pinging came again, stronger. Hail? Did they get hail in Momhilegra? There hadn't even been a cloud in the sky when she had come from the falls.

She went to the window. A liveried footman stood below her window, his hand full of pebbles. He bowed toward a carriage when she came to the window, and swept his hand toward it. There was a beautiful horse drawn carriage, the passenger spaces filled with flowers.

She raced down the steps, hoping Ryan would step out from behind the horses, but Ryan was nowhere to be seen.

The footman smiled. "Where would you like these, miss?"

She gawked at him. "For me?" she breathed.

His smile deepened with that age-old delight everyone takes in a romance.

"Yes, miss, for you."

By the time they had hauled the flowers in, every single surface in her quarters held jugs and jars of the most exquisite roses, orchids, daisies and dozens of flowers she could not name.

She didn't have enough vases. She was going to have to put flowers in the toilet bowl in a minute! But before she could, she heard the ping at the window again. This time she raced to her sill.

She looked out and that awful little pony was standing there, his headstall being held firmly by the same footman.

She ran down the stairs. The pony gave her a look of distinct dislike, but it was his cargo she was interested in. His cart was filled with chocolate—chocolate in heart-shaped containers, bricks of chocolate, chocolate carved into swans and tigers and elephants.

"Where would you like it, miss?"

Oh, if she ate all that she would be bigger than a barn! Eventually she would give it all away, but for now, she just wanted to savor this moment. Lugging as much chocolate as she could hold she retreated to her quarters.

Ping, ping. Ping, ping, ping. Ping. Ping.

The Royal Cat was in the courtyard in all its purple majesty, and when she got down there, she saw a beautiful velvet box in the front seat. She opened it and a necklace of the deepest green emeralds—a perfect match for her new gown and her eyes—winked at her.

"Okay," she said to the footman. "Tell him that's enough. I want to see him."

But the man who had guarded the necklace only laughed, happy to be part of the conspiracy.

Night was falling when she next heard the pebbles.

She ran to the window, only to find the courtyard empty. Was Ryan finally going to make an appearance? She rushed down to see, but the prince nowhere to be seen.

And then a huge boom, like a gun shot—no, more like a cannon shot—made her nearly jump out of her skin.

The sky lit up as a red comet exploded into a thousand red and white stars right over the castle. The staff were coming out of the house, Idelle and the children joined her.

"What is going on?" she said. "Is this part of the Derby?"

"Oh no, the Derby ended yesterday officially with the ball."

Ronald approached her, and bowed. He handed her a creamy piece of thick stationery.

"For you," was all the card said, in bold writing. And the next firework exploded, and the next and the next.

Everyone in the castle was now in the courtyard oohing and aahing as the sky exploded with the lights of a thousand loves.

The excitement finally died down, but not the whispers, and the secretive glances at her.

Ronald sidled up to her.

"I am to suggest you put on the green gown, miss."

"Tell him to stop it! I just want to see him. Tell him—"

"For once," Ronald said with a sigh, "couldn't you just do as you're told?"

She put her hands on her hips, ready to make a stand, but then she laughed. "Okay. But don't let him think it's going to be a habit."

"Believe me, miss, I don't think he has any illusions."

It was true Ryan had no illusions about her. And he was doing this anyway.

She went into her room and put on the green gown, and the emerald necklace. It flashed at her throat like fire, and made her eyes look more beautiful than they had ever looked.

The pebbles sounded at her window, and this time when she looked out, a highway man gazed at her window, seated on a prancing, snorting black horse.

"Why, the queen is coaching him," she guessed. The queen and Ronald, all of them loving her into the amazing Momhilegra family.

Ryan swept off his hat and bowed to her when she appeared at the window. She raced down the steps, and he held out his hand to her from the saddle.

"It'll ruin the gown," she protested. "Real horses are, well, sweaty!"

"This is no time to be pragmatic," he said sternly. "For God's sake, Prue, I'm in the middle of wooing you."

"You don't have to. Ryan, I tried to find you. I wanted to tell you—"

But he lifted a gloved hand to his lips and then held it out to her. She took it, but anybody who thought it was wildly romantic to ride a horse in a gown needed their head examined.

First the horse shied from the wind picking up her green

billowing skirts, then she heard a distinct rip as Ryan finally managed to get her up behind him on a horse that was doing rather frightening lunges sideways.

"I'm not one of those dainty little girls you can just swing onto the back of a horse," she gasped.

"Shhh," he said, but breathlessly. "Hang on."

Anybody who thought riding behind a man on a galloping horse in the dark over uneven ground was crazy.

She was terrified. She clung to him like a burr. She begged him to slow down, but he did not.

When he finally did, she recognized where they were. They were at the head of the forest pathway that led to Myria Falls.

"Do I hear music?" she asked. Of course she did. You always heard music on Momhilegra.

But here? In the middle of nowhere, in the middle of a mountain meadow? As the horse picked his way down the forest pathway in the dark, the sound of the music grew louder.

And then they entered the grotto below Myria Falls. Hundreds of candles floated in the pool, and dozens of torches illuminated the clearing. She could see a full orchestra, in tuxedos, seated among the trees, their music lit by candlelight. They were filling the grotto with the most haunting and lovely music she had ever heard.

Ryan slipped from the saddle, reached and put his hands around her waist, gave a little grunt of exertion as he lifted her down.

"That's the most beautiful music," she whispered.

"The song is called My Thousand Loves."

He went down on his knee before her.

"Ryan," she hissed, "get up. This can't be happening to me!"

"No, I'm not getting up! I want you to know this—you have become my thousand loves. Each breath you take, each smile you bestow, each beat of your heart becomes one of my thousand loves."

She realized his words were like poetry, and she could bare the emotion no longer. She began to weep.

"I know I am not a perfect man," he said softly. "I know I have terrible toes, and hairy knuckles, and that I can be unbearably arrogant at times. I know I have no talent for building go-carts and less for changing diapers."

When she tried to protest, he held up his hand and continued. "But I am asking, if even with all those imperfections, you will consider me to be your husband. To be your thousand loves over thousands of days, I am asking you, Morun—my secret love—if you will marry me."

"Ryan," she breathed.

"It's a yes or no answer," he coached her tenderly.

"Of course yes!" And he was up swinging her around in his arms, and her dress flying made the horse nervous and he crashed into the cellist and the music stopped.

And for a moment there was complete silence, candles, stars and their love filling the grotto to overflowing.

And then the applause began and thundered into the night and the champagne corks popped, and she looked into his eyes and saw everything she ever needed right there.

And then she laughed out loud and threw herself against him.

And recognized the most astounding truth within herself.

She had loved every moment of being wooed.

But she had loved those days of building the go-cart just as much.

And so love gave her this final gift of knowledge and self-understanding: it showed the girl who had once been rich that it was love that made the world special, not the things that were in that world. And it was the way your heart felt, not the amount of money you had that made you feel rich or poor. It was the song your soul sang when it looked into the eyes of another, not a title, that made a man and a woman into a prince and a princess.

* * * * *

Turn the page for a sneak preview of
IF I'D NEVER KNOWN YOUR LOVE
by
Georgia Bockoven

From the brand-new series
Harlequin Everlasting Love
Every great love has a story to tell.™

One year, five months and four days missing

There's no way for you to know this, Evan, but I haven't written to you for a few months. Actually, it's been almost a year. I had a hard time picking up a pen once more after we paid the second ransom and then received a letter saying it wasn't enough. I was so sure you were coming home that I took the kids along to Bogotá so they could fly home with you and me, something I swore I'd never do. I've fallen in love with Colombia and the people who've opened their hearts to me. But fear is a constant companion when I'm there. I won't ever expose our children to that kind of danger again.

I'm at a loss over what to do anymore, Evan. I've begged and pleaded and thrown temper tantrums with every official I can corner both here and at home.

They've been incredibly tolerant and understanding, but in the end as ineffectual as the rest of us.

I try to imagine what your life is like now, what you do every day, what you're wearing, what you eat. I want to believe that the people who have you are misguided yet kind, that they treat you well. It's how I survive day to day. To think of you being mistreated hurts too much. If I picture you locked away somewhere and suffering, a weight descends on me that makes it almost impossible to get out of bed in the morning.

Your captors surely know you by now. They have to recognize what a good man you are. I imagine you working with their children, telling them that you have children, too, showing them the pictures you carry in your wallet. Can't the men who have you understand how much your children miss you? How can it not matter to them?

How can they keep you away from us all this time? Over and over, we've done what they asked. Are they oblivious to the depth of their cruelty? What kind of people are they that they don't care?

I used to keep a calendar beside our bed next to the peach rose you picked for me before you left. Every night I marked another day, counting how many you'd been gone. I don't do that any longer. I don't want to be reminded of all the days we'll never get back.

When I can't sleep at night, I tell you about my day. I imagine you hearing me and smiling over the details that make up my life now. I never tell you how defeated I feel at moments or how hard I work to hide it from everyone for fear they will see it as a reason to stop believing you are coming home to us.

And I couldn't tell you about the lump I found in my

breast and how difficult it was going through all the tests without you here to lean on. The lump was benign— the process reaching that diagnosis utterly terrifying. I couldn't stop thinking about what would happen to Shelly and Jason if something happened to me.

We need you to come home.

I'm worn down with missing you.

I'm going to read this tomorrow and will probably tear it up or burn it in the fireplace. I don't want you to get the idea I ever doubted what I was doing to free you or thought the work a burden. I would gladly spend the rest of my life at it, even if, in the end, we only had one day together.

You are my life, Evan.

I will love you forever.

* * * * *

Don't miss this deeply moving Harlequin Everlasting Love story about a woman's struggle to bring back her kidnapped husband from Colombia and her turmoil over whether to let go, finally, and welcome another man into her life.
IF I'D NEVER KNOWN YOUR LOVE
by Georgia Bockoven
is available March 27, 2007.

And also look for
THE NIGHT WE MET
by Tara Taylor Quinn,
a story about finding love when you least expect it.

AMERICAN *Romance*®

Babies, babies, babies!

If one baby is delightful, just imagine life with two!

In Laura Marie Altom's *Babies and Badges*, Arkansas sheriff Noah Wheeler finds himself with not one but two babes in arms when he renders roadside assistance to Cassie Tremont and discovers her in the throes of labor. Once she gives birth to twins, Noah falls for these fatherless infants—and he falls just as hard for their gorgeous mother....

Available in July 2004 wherever Harlequin books are sold.

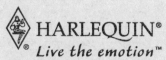

AMERICAN Baby

HARLEQUIN®
Live the emotion™

www.americanromances.com

HARAB

Discover the power of body language
as Harlequin Blaze goes international
with the new miniseries
LUST IN TRANSLATION!

This April, reader-favorite Jamie Sobrato
takes us to Italy in search of the
perfect lover in

SEX AS
A SECOND
LANGUAGE

Look for more
LUST IN TRANSLATION
books from Nancy Warren in June 2007
and Kate Hoffmann in August 2007!

www.eHarlequin.com   HB316

REQUEST YOUR FREE BOOKS!
2 FREE NOVELS PLUS 2
FREE GIFTS!

HARLEQUIN ROMANCE®

From the Heart, For the Heart

YES! Please send me 2 FREE Harlequin Romance® novels and my 2 FREE gifts. After receiving them, if I don't wish to receive any more books, I can return the shipping statement marked "cancel." If I don't cancel, I will receive 4 brand-new novels every month and be billed just $3.57 per book in the U.S., or $4.05 per book in Canada, plus 25¢ shipping and handling per book and applicable taxes, if any*. That's a savings of over 15% off the cover price! I understand that accepting the 2 free books and gifts places me under no obligation to buy anything. I can always return a shipment and cancel at any time. Even if I never buy another book from Harlequin, the two free books and gifts are mine to keep forever.

114 HDN EEV7 314 HDN EEWK

Name	(PLEASE PRINT)

Address	Apt.

City	State/Prov.	Zip/Postal Code

Signature (if under 18, a parent or guardian must sign)

Mail to the **Harlequin Reader Service®**:
IN U.S.A.: P.O. Box 1867, Buffalo, NY 14240-1867
IN CANADA: P.O. Box 609, Fort Erie, Ontario L2A 5X3

Not valid to current Harlequin Romance subscribers.

Want to try two free books from another line?
Call 1-800-873-8635 or visit www.morefreebooks.com.

* Terms and prices subject to change without notice. NY residents add applicable sales tax. Canadian residents will be charged applicable provincial taxes and GST. This offer is limited to one order per household. All orders subject to approval. Credit or debit balances in a customer's account(s) may be offset by any other outstanding balance owed by or to the customer. Please allow 4 to 6 weeks for delivery.

Your Privacy: Harlequin is committed to protecting your privacy. Our Privacy Policy is available online at www.eHarlequin.com or upon request from the Reader Service. From time to time we make our lists of customers available to reputable firms who may have a product or service of interest to you. If you would prefer we not share your name and address, please check here. ☐

HR07

Coming Next Month

#3943 RAISING THE RANCHER'S FAMILY Patricia Thayer
Rocky Mountain Brides
New York tycoon Holt Rawlins is back home in Destiny to find the truth, not to make friends. But when beautiful Leah Keenan bursts into his life, Holt finds he cannot let her go. Leah knows that soon she will have to return to her old life, but to leave Holt will break her heart. Will the rugged rancher persuade her to stay?

#3944 MATRIMONY WITH HIS MAJESTY Rebecca Winters
By Royal Appointment
Darrell Collier is an ordinary single mom. Alexander Valleder is a good, responsible king. But one night, years ago, he rebelled a little. The result, as he's just discovered, was a child. Now Alex has to sweep Darrell off her feet and persuade her that she has the makings of a queen.

#3945 THE SHEIKH'S RELUCTANT BRIDE Teresa Southwick
Desert Brides
Jessica Sterling has just discovered that in the desert kingdom of Bha'Khar is the man that she has been betrothed to since birth! Sheikh Kardhal Hourani is rich, gorgeous and arrogant. Can Jessica see the man behind the playboy persona and find her way into his guarded heart?

#3946 IN THE HEART OF THE OUTBACK… Barbara Hannay
Byrne Drummond has every reason to hate Fiona McLaren—her reckless brother destroyed his family. But the image of Byrne has been etched in Fiona's mind ever since she first saw the stoic, broad-shouldered cattleman. And Fiona's touch is the first to draw him in years.

#3947 MARRIAGE FOR BABY Melissa McClone
Career-driven couple Jared and Katie have separated. But when they find themselves guardians of an orphaned baby they agree to give their marriage another go for the sake of the child. Little do they know how much this tiny baby will turn their lives—and marriage—upside down.

#3948 RESCUED: MOTHER-TO-BE Trish Wylie
Baby on Board
Colleen McKenna knew that she would have to be strong to cope with her pregnancy alone. But now gorgeous millionaire Eamonn Murphy's kindness is testing her fierce independence. And having Eamonn share each tiny kick with her makes each moment more special than the last.

HRCNM0307